ISBN 978-1-330-41939-7
PIBN 10058899

This book is a reproduction of an important historical work. Forgotten Books uses state-of-the-art technology to digitally reconstruct the work, preserving the original format whilst repairing imperfections present in the aged copy. In rare cases, an imperfection in the original, such as a blemish or missing page, may be replicated in our edition. We do, however, repair the vast majority of imperfections successfully; any imperfections that remain are intentionally left to preserve the state of such historical works.

1 MONTH OF
FREE
READING

at

www.ForgottenBooks.com

By purchasing this book you are eligible for one month membership to ForgottenBooks.com, giving you unlimited access to our entire collection of over 700,000 titles via our web site and mobile apps.

To claim your free month visit:

www.forgottenbooks.com/free58899

English
Français
Deutsche
Italiano
Español
Português

www.forgottenbooks.com

Mythology Photography **Fiction**
Fishing Christianity **Art** Cooking
Essays Buddhism Freemasonry
Medicine **Biology** Music **Ancient
Egypt** Evolution Carpentry Physics
Dance Geology **Mathematics** Fitness
Shakespeare **Folklore** Yoga Marketing
Confidence Immortality Biographies
Poetry **Psychology** Witchcraft
Electronics Chemistry History **Law**
Accounting **Philosophy** Anthropology
Alchemy Drama Quantum Mechanics
Atheism Sexual Health **Ancient History**
Entrepreneurship Languages Sport
Paleontology Needlework Islam
Metaphysics Investment Archaeology
Parenting Statistics Criminology
Motivational

THE STRANGE CASE OF DR. JEKYLL AND MR. HYDE

WITH OTHER FABLES

WORKS BY ROBERT LOUIS STEVENSON

LETTERS TO HIS FAMILY AND FRIENDS. Selected
   and Edited by SIDNEY COLVIN. 2 Vols.
AN INLAND VOYAGE
EDINBURGH: PICTURESQUE NOTES
TRAVELS WITH A DONKEY
VIRGINIBUS PUERISQUE
FAMILIAR STUDIES OF MEN AND BOOKS
NEW ARABIAN NIGHTS
THE ADVENTURES OF DAVID BALFOUR—
    Part I.—KIDNAPPED
    Part II.—CATRIONA
THE BLACK ARROW
THE MASTER OF BALLANTRAE
ISLAND NIGHTS' ENTERTAINMENTS
A FOOTNOTE TO HISTORY
TREASURE ISLAND
THE SILVERADO SQUATTERS
A CHILD'S GARDEN OF VERSES
STRANGE CASE OF DR. JEKYLL AND MR. HYDE·
    WITH OTHER FABLES
PRINCE OTTO
THE MERRY MEN
BALLADS
UNDERWOODS
ACROSS THE PLAINS
MEMORIES AND PORTRAITS
FATHER DAMIEN
THE SUICIDE CLUB: and THE RAJAH'S DIAMOND
     (From NEW ARABIAN NIGHTS)
VAILIMA LETTERS
SONGS OF TRAVEL
LOWDEN SABBATH MORN
WEIR OF HERMISTON
IN THE SOUTH SEAS

(WITH MRS. STEVENSON)
MORE NEW ARABIAN NIGHTS: THE DYNAMITER

(WITH LLOYD OSBOURNE)
THE WRONG BOX
THE WRECKER
THE EBB-TIDE

(WITH A. T. Q. COUCH)
ST. IVES

THE STRANGE CASE

OF

DR. JEKYLL AND MR. HYDE

WITH OTHER FABLES

.

BY

ROBERT LOUIS STEVENSON

NEW IMPRESSION

LONGMANS, GREEN, AND CO.

39 PATERNOSTER ROW, LONDON

NEW YORK, BOMBAY, AND CALCUTTA

1911

BIBLIOGRAPHICAL NOTE.

First Edition, December, 1885.
Twenty-sixth Impression, October, 1907.
With other Fables, March, 1896.
"Silver Library" Edition, March, 1896.
Reprinted, March, 1897; *September,* 1898; *April,* 1901;
October, 1903; *March,* 1906.
Reprinted uniform with other Works, September, 1901,
and January, 1909.
Pocket Library Edition, December, 1906.
Reprinted, January, 1907; *June,* 1907;
September, 1908; *and January,* 1911.

CONTENTS.

THE STRANGE CASE OF DR. JEKYLL AND MR. HYDE

FABLES.

THE STRANGE CASE

OF

DR. JEKYLL AND MR. HYDE.

STORY OF THE DOOR.

MR. UTTERSON the lawyer was a man of a rugged countenance, that was never lighted by a smile; cold, scanty and embarrassed in discourse; backward in sentiment; lean, long, dusty, dreary, and yet somehow lovable. At friendly meetings, and when the wine was to his taste, something eminently human beaconed from his eye; something indeed which never found its way into his talk, but which spoke not only in these silent symbols of the after-dinner face, but more often and loudly in the acts of his life. He was austere with himself; drank gin when he was alone, to mortify a taste for vintages; and though he enjoyed the theatre, had not crossed the doors of one for twenty years. But he had an approved tolerance for others; sometimes wondering, almost with envy, at the high pressure of spirits involved in their misdeeds; and in any extremity inclined to help rather than to reprove. "I incline to Cain's heresy," he used to say quaintly: "I let my brother go to the devil in his own way." In this character, it was frequently his fortune to be the last reputable acquaintance and the last good influence in the lives of down-going men. And to such as these, so long as they came about his chambers, he never marked a shade of change in his demeanour.

No doubt the feat was easy to Mr. Utterson; for he was undemonstrative at the best, and even his friendships seemed to be founded in a similar catholicity of good-nature. It is the mark of a modest man to accept his friendly circle ready made from the hands of opportunity; and that was the lawyer's way. His friends were those of his own blood, or those whom he had known the longest; his affections, like ivy, were the growth of time, they implied no aptness in the object. Hence, no doubt, the bond that united him to Mr. Richard Enfield, his distant kinsman, the well-known man about town. It was a nut to crack for many, what these two could see in each other, or what subject they could find in common. It was reported by those who encountered them in their Sunday walks, that they said nothing, looked singularly dull, and would hail with obvious relief the appearance of a friend. For all that, the two men put the greatest store by these excursions, counted them the chief jewel of each week, and not only set aside occasions of pleasure, but even resisted the calls of business, that they might enjoy them uninterrupted.

It chanced on one of these rambles that their way led them down a by-street in a busy quarter of London. The street was small and what is called quiet, but it drove a thriving trade on the week-days. The

inhabitants were all doing well, it seemed,
and all emulously hoping to do better still,
and laying out the surplus of their gains in
coquetry ; so that the shop fronts stood along
that thoroughfare with an air of invitation, like
rows of smiling saleswomen.   Even on Sunday, when it veiled its more florid charms
and lay comparatively empty of passage, the
street shone out in contrast to its dingy neighbourhood, like a fire in a forest ; and with its
freshly painted shutters, well-polished brasses,
and general cleanliness and gaiety of note,
instantly caught and pleased the eye of the
passenger.

Two doors from one corner, on the left
hand going east, the line was broken by the
entry of a court ; and just at that point, a
certain sinister block of building thrust forward its gable on the street.   It was two
storeys high ; showed no window, nothing
but a door on the lower storey and a blind
forehead of discoloured wall on the upper ;
and bore in every feature the marks of pro-
longed and sordid negligence.   The door,

which was equipped with neither bell nor knocker, was blistered and distained. Tramps slouched into the recess and struck matches on the panels; children kept shop upon the steps; the schoolboy had tried his knife on the mouldings; and for close on a generation, no one had appeared to drive away these random visitors or to repair their ravages.

Mr. Enfield and the lawyer were on the other side of the by-street; but when they came abreast of the entry, the former lifted up his cane and pointed.

"Did you ever remark that door?" he asked; and when his companion had replied in the affirmative, "It is connected in my mind," added he, "with a very odd story".

"Indeed!" said Mr. Utterson, with a slight change of voice, "and what was that?"

"Well, it was this way," returned Mr. Enfield: "I was coming home from some place at the end of the world, about three o'clock of a black winter morning, and my way lay through a part of town where there was liter-

ally nothing to be seen but lamps. Street
after street, and all the folks asleep—street
after street, all lighted up as if for a procession, and all as empty as a church—till at last
I got into that state of mind when a man
listens and listens and begins to long for the
sight of a policeman. All at once, I saw two
figures : one a little man who was stumping
along eastward at a good walk, and the other
a girl of maybe eight or ten who was running
as hard as she was able down a cross street.
Well, sir, the two ran into one another
naturally enough at the corner; and then
came the horrible part of the thing ; for the
man trampled calmly over the child's body
and left her screaming on the ground. It
sounds nothing to hear, but it was hellish to
see. It wasn't like a man ; it was like some
damned Juggernaut. I gave a view halloa,
took to my heels, collared my gentleman, and
brought him back to where there was already
quite a group about the screaming child. He
was perfectly cool and made no resistance,
but gave me one look, so ugly that it brought

out the sweat on me like running. The
people who had turned out were the girl's
own family; and pretty soon the doctor, for
whom she had been sent, put in his appearance. Well, the child was not much the
worse, more frightened, according to the
Sawbones; and there you might have supposed would be an end to it. But there was
one curious circumstance. I had taken a
loathing to my gentleman at first sight. So
had the child's family, which was only natural.
But the doctor's case was what struck me.
He was the usual cut and dry apothecary, of
no particular age and colour, with a strong
Edinburgh accent, and about as emotional
as a bagpipe. Well, sir, he was like the rest
of us; every time he looked at my prisoner,
I saw that Sawbones turned sick and white
with the desire to kill him. I knew what
was in his mind, just as he knew what was
in mine; and killing being out of the question, we did the next best. We told the man
we could and would make such a scandal out
of this, as should make his name stink from

one end of London to the other.   If he had
any friends or any credit, we undertook that
he should lose them.   And all the time, as
we were pitching it in red hot, we were keep-
ing the women off him as best we could, for
they were as wild as harpies.   I never saw
a circle of such hateful faces; and there was
the man in the middle, with a kind of black,
sneering coolness—frightened too, I could
see that—but carrying it off, sir, really like
Satan.   'If you choose to make capital out
of this accident,' said he, 'I am naturally
helpless.   No gentleman but wishes to avoid
a scene,' says he.   'Name your figure.'
Well, we screwed him up to a hundred pounds
for the child's family; he would have clearly
liked to stick out; but there was something
about the lot of us that meant mischief, and
at last he struck.   The next thing was to
get the money; and where do you think he
carried us but to that place with the door?
—whipped out a key, went in, and presently
came back with the matter of ten pounds in
gold and a cheque for the balance on Coutts's,

drawn payable to bearer, and signed with a name that I can't mention, though it's one of the points of my story, but it was a name at least very well known and often printed. The figure was stiff; but the signature was good for more than that, if it was only genuine. I took the liberty of pointing out to my gentleman that the whole business looked apocryphal; and that a man does not, in real life, walk into a cellar door at four in the morning and come out of it with another man's cheque for close upon a hundred pounds. But he was quite easy and sneering. 'Set your mind at rest,' says he; 'I will stay with you till the banks open, and cash the cheque myself.' So we all set off, the doctor, and the child's father, and our friend and myself, and passed the rest of the night in my chambers; and next day, when we had breakfasted, went in a body to the bank. I gave in the cheque myself, and said I had every reason to believe it was a forgery. Not a bit of it. The cheque was genuine."

"Tut-tut!" said Mr. Utterson.

"I see you feel as I do," said Mr. Enfield. "Yes, it's a bad story. For my man was a fellow that nobody could have to do with, a really damnable man; and the person that drew the cheque is the very pink of the proprieties, celebrated too, and (what makes it worse) one of your fellows who do what they call good. Black mail, I suppose; an honest man paying through the nose for some of the capers of his youth. Black Mail House is what I call that place with the door, in consequence. Though even that, you know, is far from explaining all," he added; and with the words fell into a vein of musing.

From this he was recalled by Mr. Utterson asking rather suddenly: "And you don't know if the drawer of the cheque lives there?"

"A likely place, isn't it?" returned Mr. Enfield. "But I happen to have noticed his address; he lives in some square or other."

"And you never asked about—the place with the door?" said Mr. Utterson.

"No, sir: I had a delicacy," was the reply. "I feel very strongly about putting questions; it partakes too much of the style of the day of judgment. You start a question, and it's like starting a stone. You sit quietly on the top of a hill; and away the stone goes, starting others; and presently some bland old bird (the last you would have thought of) is knocked on the head in his own back garden, and the family have to change their name. No, sir, I make it a rule of mine: the more it looks like Queer Street, the less I ask."

"A very good rule, too," said the lawyer.

"But I have studied the place for myself," continued Mr. Enfield. "It seems scarcely a house. There is no other door, and nobody goes in or out of that one, but, once in a great while, the gentleman of my adventure. There are three windows looking on the court on the first floor; none below; the windows are always shut, but they're clean. And then there is a chimney, which is generally smoking; so somebody must live there. And yet it's not so sure; for the buildings are so packed together about that court, that it's hard to say where one ends and another begins."

The pair walked on again for a while in silence; and then—"Enfield," said Mr. Utterson, "that's a good rule of yours".

"Yes, I think it is," returned Enfield.

"But for all that," continued the lawyer, "there's one point I want to ask: I want to ask the name of that man who walked over the child."

"Well," said Mr. Enfield, "I can't see what harm it would do. It was a man of the name of Hyde."

"Hm," said Mr. Utterson. "What sort of a man is he to see?"

"He is not easy to describe. There is something wrong with his appearance; something displeasing, something downright detestable. I never saw a man I so disliked, and yet I scarce know why. He must be deformed somewhere; he gives a strong feeling of deformity, although I couldn't specify the point. He's an extraordinary looking man, and yet I really can name nothing out of the way. No, sir; I can make no hand of it; I can't describe him. And it's not want of memory; for I declare I can see him this moment."

Mr. Utterson again walked some way in silence, and obviously under a weight of consideration. "You are sure he used a key?" he inquired at last.

"My dear sir . . ." began Enfield, surprised out of himself.

"Yes, I know," said Utterson; "I know it must seem strange. The fact is, if I do not ask you the name of the other party, it is because I know it already. You see, Richard, your tale has gone home. If you have been inexact in any point, you had better correct it."

"I think you might have warned me," returned the other, with a touch of sullen-ness. "But I have been pedantically exact, as you call it. The fellow had a key; and, what's more, he has it still. I saw him use it, not a week ago."

Mr. Utterson sighed deeply, but said never a word; and the young man presently resumed. "Here is another lesson to say nothing," said he. "I am ashamed of my long tongue. Let us make a bargain never to refer to this again."

"With all my heart," said the lawyer. "I shake hands on that, Richard."

SEARCH FOR MR. HYDE.

THAT evening Mr. Utterson came home to his bachelor house in sombre spirits, and sat down to dinner without relish. It was his custom of a Sunday, when this meal was over, to sit close by the fire, a volume of some dry divinity on his reading desk, until the clock of the neighbouring church rang out the hour of twelve, when he would go soberly and gratefully to bed. On this night, however, as soon as the cloth was taken away, he took up a candle and went into his business room. There he opened his safe, took from the most private part of it a document endorsed on the envelope as Dr. Jekyll's Will, and sat down with a clouded brow to study its contents. The will was holograph ; for Mr. Utterson, though he took charge of it now that it was made, had refused to lend the least assistance in the making of it; it provided not only that, in case of the decease of Henry Jekyll, M.D., D.C.L., LL.D., F.R.S., etc., all his possessions were to pass into the hands of his "friend and benefactor Edward Hyde"; but that in case of Dr. Jekyll's "disappearance or unexplained absence for any period exceeding three calendar months," the said Edward Hyde should step into the said Henry Jekyll's shoes without further delay, and free from any burthen or obligation, beyond the payment of a few small sums to the members of the doctor's household. This document had long been the lawyer's eyesore. It offended him both as a lawyer and as a lover of the sane and customary sides of life, to whom the fanciful was the immodest. And hitherto it was his ignorance of Mr. Hyde that had swelled his indignation; now, by a sudden turn, it was his knowledge. It was already bad enough when the name was but a name of which he could learn no more. It was worse when it began to be clothed upon with detestable attributes; and out of the shifting, insubstantial mists that had so long baffled his eye, there leaped up the sudden, definite presentment of a fiend.

"I thought it was madness," he said, as he replaced the obnoxious paper in the safe; "and now I begin to fear it is disgrace."

With that he blew out his candle, put on a great coat, and set forth in the direction of Cavendish Square, that citadel of medicine, where his friend, the great Dr. Lanyon, had his house and received his crowding patients. "If any one knows, it will be Lanyon," he had thought.

The solemn butler knew and welcomed him; he was subjected to no stage of delay, but ushered direct from the door to the dining-room, where Dr. Lanyon sat alone over his wine. This was a hearty, healthy, dapper, red-faced gentleman, with a shock of hair prematurely white, and a boisterous and decided manner. At sight of Mr. Utterson, he sprang up from his chair and welcomed him with both hands. The geniality, as was

the way of the man, was somewhat theatrical
to the eye; but it reposed on genuine feeling.
For these two were old friends, old mates
both at school and college, both thorough
respecters of themselves and of each other,
and, what does not always follow, men who
thoroughly enjoyed each other's company.

After a little rambling talk, the lawyer led
up to the subject which so disagreeably
preoccupied his mind.

"I suppose, Lanyon," said he, "you and I
must be the two oldest friends that Henry
Jekyll has?"

"I wish the friends were younger," chuckled
Dr. Lanyon. "But I suppose we are. And
what of that? I see little of him now."

"Indeed!" said Utterson. "I thought you
had a bond of common interest."

"We had," was the reply. "But it is more
than ten years since Henry Jekyll became
too fanciful for me. He began to go wrong,
wrong in mind; and though, of course, I continue to take an interest in him for old sake's
sake as they say, I see and I have seen

devilish little of the man. Such unscien-
tific balderdash," added the doctor, flushing
suddenly purple, "would have estranged
Damon and Pythias."

This little spirt of temper was somewhat
of a relief to Mr. Utterson. "They have
only differed on some point of science," he
thought; and being a man of no scientific
passions (except in the matter of conveyanc-
ing) he even added: "It is nothing worse
than that!" He gave his friend a few
seconds to recover his composure, and then
approached the question he had come to put.

"Did you ever come across a *protégé*
of his—one Hyde?" he asked.

"Hyde?" repeated Lanyon. "No. Never
heard of him. Since my time."

That was the amount of information that
the lawyer carried back with him to the
great, dark bed on which he tossed to and
fro, until the small hours of the morning began to grow large. It was a night of little
ease to his toiling mind, toiling in mere
darkness and besieged by questions.

Six o'clock struck on the bells of the church that was so conveniently near to Mr. Utterson's dwelling, and still he was digging at the problem. Hitherto it had touched him on the intellectual side alone; but now his imagination also was engaged, or rather enslaved; and as he lay and tossed in the gross darkness of the night and the curtained room, Mr. Enfield's tale went by before his mind in a scroll of lighted pictures. He would be aware of the great field of lamps of a nocturnal city; then of the figure of a man walking swiftly; then of a child running from the doctor's; and then these met, and that human Juggernaut trod the child down and passed on regardless of her screams. Or else he would see a room in a rich house, where his friend lay asleep, dreaming and smiling at his dreams; and then the door of that room would be opened, the curtains of the bed plucked apart, the sleeper recalled, and, lo! there would stand by his side a figure to whom power was given, and even at that dead hour, he must rise and do its bidding. The figure in these two phases haunted the lawyer all night; and if at any time he dozed over, it was but to see it glide more stealthily through sleeping houses, or move the more swiftly and still the more swiftly, even to dizziness, through wider labyrinths of lamp-lighted city, and at every street corner crush a child and leave her screaming. And still the figure had no face by which he might know it; even in his dreams, it had no face, or one that baffled him and melted before his eyes; and thus it was that there sprang up and grew apace in the lawyer's mind a singularly strong, almost an inordinate, curiosity to behold the features of the real Mr. Hyde. If he could but once set eyes on him, he thought the mystery would lighten and perhaps roll altogether away, as was the habit of mysterious things when well examined. He might see a reason for his friend's strange preference or bondage (call it which you please), and even for the startling clauses of the will. And at least it would be a face worth seeing: the face of a man who

was without bowels of mercy : a face which
had but to show itself to raise up, in the
mind of the unimpressionable Enfield, a
spirit of enduring hatred.

From that time forward, Mr. Utterson began to haunt the door in the by-street of
shops.   In the morning before office hours,
at noon when business was plenty and time
scarce, at night under the face of the fogged
city moon, by all lights and at all hours of
solitude or concourse, the lawyer was to be
found on his chosen post.

"If he be Mr. Hyde," he had thought,
"I shall be Mr. Seek."

And at last his patience was rewarded.
It was a fine dry night; frost in the air;
the streets as clean as a ball-room floor;
the lamps, unshaken by any wind, drawing
a regular pattern of light and shadow.   By
ten o'clock, when the shops were closed, the
by-street was very solitary, and, in spite of
the low growl of London from all round, very
silent.   Small sounds carried far ; domestic
sounds out of the houses were clearly audible

on either side of the roadway; and the
rumour of the approach of any passenger
preceded him by a long time. Mr. Utterson
had been some minutes at his post when he
was aware of an odd, light footstep drawing
near. In the course of his nightly patrols
he had long grown accustomed to the quaint
effect with which the footfalls of a single
person, while he is still a great way off,
suddenly spring out distinct from the vast
hum and clatter of the city. Yet his attention had never before been so sharply and
decisively arrested; and it was with a strong,
superstitious prevision of success that he
withdrew into the entry of the court.

The steps drew swiftly nearer, and swelled
out suddenly louder as they turned the end
of the street. The lawyer, looking forth
from the entry, could soon see what manner
of man he had to deal with. He was small,
and very plainly dressed; and the look of
him, even at that distance, went somehow
strongly against the watcher's inclination.
But he made straight for the door, crossing

the roadway to save time; and as he came, he drew a key from his pocket, like one approaching home.

Mr. Utterson stepped out and touched him on the shoulder as he passed. "Mr. Hyde, I think?"

Mr. Hyde shrank back with a hissing intake of the breath. But his fear was only momentary; and though he did not look the lawyer in the face, he answered coolly enough: "That is my name. What do you want?"

"I see you are going in," returned the lawyer. "I am an old friend of Dr. Jekyll's —Mr. Utterson, of Gaunt Street—you must have heard my name; and meeting you so conveniently, I thought you might admit me."

"You will not find Dr. Jekyll; he is from home," replied Mr. Hyde, blowing in the key. And then suddenly, but still without looking up, "How did you know me?" he asked.

"On your side," said Mr. Utterson, "will you do me a favour?"

"With pleasure," replied the other. "What shall it be?"

"Will you let me see your face?" asked the lawyer.

Mr. Hyde appeared to hesitate; and then, as if upon some sudden reflection, fronted about with an air of defiance; and the pair stared at each other pretty fixedly for a few seconds. "Now I shall know you again," said Mr. Utterson. "It may be useful."

"Yes," returned Mr. Hyde, "it is as well we have met; and *à propos*, you should have my address." And he gave a number of a street in Soho.

"Good God!" thought Mr. Utterson, "can he too have been thinking of the will?" But he kept his feelings to himself, and only grunted in acknowledgment of the address.

"And now," said the other, "how did you know me?"

"By description," was the reply.

"Whose description?"

"We have common friends," said Mr. Utterson.

"Common friends!" echoed Mr. Hyde, a little hoarsely. "Who are they?"

"Jekyll, for instance," said the lawyer.

"He never told you," cried Mr. Hyde, with a flush of anger. "I did not think you would have lied."

"Come," said Mr. Utterson, "that is not fitting language."

The other snarled aloud into a savage laugh; and the next moment, with extraordinary quickness, he had unlocked the door and disappeared into the house.

The lawyer stood awhile when Mr. Hyde had left him, the picture of disquietude. Then he began slowly to mount the street, pausing every step or two, and putting his hand to his brow like a man in mental perplexity. The problem he was thus debating as he walked was one of a class that is rarely solved. Mr. Hyde was pale and dwarfish; he gave an impression of deformity without any namable malformation, he had a displeasing smile, he had borne himself to the lawyer with a sort of murderous mixture of timidity and boldness, and he spoke with a husky, whispering and somewhat broken voice,—all these were points against him ; but not all of these together could explain the hitherto unknown disgust, loathing and fear with which Mr. Utterson regarded him. "There must be something else," said the perplexed gentleman. "There *is* something more, if I could find a name for it. God bless me, the man seems hardly human ! Something troglodytic, *x* shall we say ? or can it be the old story of Dr. Fell ? or is it the mere radiance of a foul soul that thus transpires through, and transfigures, its clay continent ? The last, I think ; for, O my poor old Harry Jekyll, if ever I read Satan's signature upon a face, } it is on that of your new friend."

Round the corner from the by-street there was a square of ancient, handsome houses, now for the most part decayed from their high estate, and let in flats and chambers, to all sorts and conditions of men : map-engravers, architects, shady lawyers, and the

agents of obscure enterprises.   One house,
however, second from the corner, was still
occupied entire ; and at the door of this,
which wore a great air of wealth and
comfort, though it was now plunged in
darkness except for the fan-light, Mr.
Utterson stopped and knocked.   A well-
dressed, elderly servant opened the door.

"Is Dr. Jekyll at home, Poole ? " asked
the lawyer.

" I will see, Mr. Utterson," said Poole, ad-
mitting the visitor, as he spoke, into a large,
low-roofed, comfortable hall, paved with
flags, warmed (after the fashion of a country
house) by a bright, open fire, and furnished
with costly cabinets of oak.   " Will you wait
here by the fire, sir ? or shall I give you a
light in the dining-room ? "

" Here, thank you," said the lawyer ; and
he drew near and leaned on the tall fender.
This hall, in which he was now left alone,
was a pet fancy of his friend the doctor's ;
and Utterson himself was wont to speak of
it as the pleasantest room in London.   But

to-night there was a shudder in his blood; the face of Hyde sat heavy on his memory; he felt (what was rare with him) a nausea and distaste of life; and in the gloom of his spirits, he seemed to read a menace in the flickering of the firelight on the polished cabinets and the uneasy starting of the shadow on the roof. He was ashamed of his relief, when Poole presently returned to announce that Dr. Jekyll was gone out.

"I saw Mr. Hyde go in by the old dissecting room door, Poole," he said. "Is that right, when Dr. Jekyll is from home?"

"Quite right, Mr. Utterson, sir," replied the servant. "Mr. Hyde has a key."

"Your master seems to repose a great deal of trust in that young man, Poole," resumed the other, musingly.

"Yes, sir, he do indeed," said Poole. "We have all orders to obey him."

"I do not think I ever met Mr. Hyde?" asked Utterson.

"O dear no, sir. He never *dines* here,"
replied the butler. "Indeed, we see very
little of him on this side of the house; he
mostly comes and goes by the laboratory."

"Well, good-night, Poole."

"Good-night, Mr. Utterson."

And the lawyer set out homeward with a
very heavy heart. "Poor Harry Jekyll,"
he thought, "my mind misgives me he is
in deep waters! He was wild when he was
young; a long while ago, to be sure; but
in the law of God, there is no statute of
limitations. Ah, it must be that; the ghost
of some old sin, the cancer of some concealed disgrace; punishment coming, *pede
claudo*, years after memory has forgotten and
self-love condoned the fault." And the
lawyer, scared by the thought, brooded
awhile on his own past, groping in all the
corners of memory, lest by chance some
Jack-in-the-Box of an old iniquity should
leap to light there. His past was fairly
blameless; few men could read the rolls of
their life with less apprehension; yet he

was humbled to the dust by the many ill things he had done, and raised up again into a sober and fearful gratitude by the many that he had come so near to doing, yet avoided. And then by a return on his former subject, he conceived a spark of hope. "This Master Hyde, if he were studied," thought he, "must have secrets of his own : black secrets, by the look of him ; secrets compared to which poor Jekyll's worst would be like sunshine. Things cannot continue as they are. It turns me cold to think of this creature stealing like a thief to Harry's bedside; poor Harry, what a wakening ! And the danger of it ! for if this Hyde suspects the existence of the will, he may grow impatient to inherit. Ah, I must put my shoulder to the wheel—if Jekyll will but let me," he added, "if Jekyll will only let me." For once more he saw before his mind's eye, as clear as a transparency, the strange clauses of the will.

DR. JEKYLL WAS QUITE AT EASE.

A FORTNIGHT later, by excellent good fortune, the doctor gave one of his pleasant dinners to some five or six old cronies, all intelligent reputable men, and all judges of good wine; and Mr. Utterson so contrived that he remained behind after the others had departed. This was no new arrangement, but a thing that had befallen many scores of times. Where Utterson was liked, he was liked well. Hosts loved to detain the dry lawyer, when the light-hearted and the loose-tongued had already their foot on the threshold; they liked to sit awhile in his unobtrusive company, practising for solitude, sobering their minds in the man's rich silence, after the expense and strain of gaiety. To this rule, Dr. Jekyll was no exception; and as he now sat on the opposite side of the fire—a large,

well-made, smooth-faced man of fifty, with
something of a slyish cast perhaps, but every
mark of capacity and kindness—you could
see by his looks that he cherished for Mr.
Utterson a sincere and warm affection.

"I have been wanting to speak to you,
Jekyll," began the latter. "You know that
will of yours?"

A close observer might have gathered that
the topic was distasteful; but the doctor
carried it off gaily. "My poor Utterson,"
said he, "you are unfortunate in such a
client. I never saw a man so distressed as
you were by my will; unless it were that
hide-bound pedant, Lanyon, at what he called
my scientific heresies. O, I know he's a
good fellow—you needn't frown—an excellent fellow, and I always mean to see more
of him; but a hide-bound pedant for all that;
an ignorant, blatant pedant. I was never
more disappointed in any man than Lanyon."

"You know I never approved of it," pur-
sued Utterson, ruthlessly disregarding the
fresh topic.

"My will? Yes, certainly, I know that," said the doctor, a trifle sharply. "You have told me so."

"Well, I tell you so again," continued the lawyer. "I have been learning something of young Hyde."

The large handsome face of Dr. Jekyll grew pale to the very lips, and there came a blackness about his eyes. "I do not care to hear more," said he. "This is a matter I thought we had agreed to drop."

"What I heard was abominable," said Utterson.

"It can make no change. You do not understand my position," returned the doctor, with a certain incoherency of manner. "I am painfully situated, Utterson ; my position is a very strange—a very strange one. It is one of those affairs that cannot be mended by talking."

"Jekyll," said Utterson, "you know me : I am a man to be trusted. Make a clean breast of this in confidence ; and I make no doubt I can get you out of it."

"My good Utterson," said the doctor, "this is very good of you, this is downright good of you, and I cannot find words to thank you in. I believe you fully; I would trust you before any man alive, ay, before myself, if I could make the choice; but indeed it isn't what you fancy; it is not so bad as that; and just to put your good heart at rest, I will tell you one thing: the moment I choose, I can be rid of Mr. Hyde. I give you my hand upon that; and I thank you again and again; and I will just add one little word, Utterson, that I'm sure you'll take in good part: this is a private matter, and I beg of you to let it sleep."

Utterson reflected a little, looking in the fire.

"I have no doubt you are perfectly right," he said at last, getting to his feet.

"Well, but since we have touched upon this business, and for the last time I hope," continued the doctor, "there is one point I should like you to understand. I have really a very great interest in poor Hyde. I know you have seen him; he told me so; and I fear he was rude. But I do sincerely take a great, a very great interest in that young man; and if I am taken away, Utterson, I wish you to promise me that you will bear with him and get his rights for him. I think you would, if you knew all; and it would be a weight off my mind if you would promise."

"I can't pretend that I shall ever like him," said the lawyer.

"I don't ask that," pleaded Jekyll, laying his hand upon the other's arm; "I only ask for justice; I only ask you to help him for my sake, when I am no longer here."

Utterson heaved an irrepressible sigh. "Well," said he, "I promise."

THE CAREW MURDER CASE.

NEARLY a year later, in the month of October, 18—, London was startled by a crime of singular ferocity, and rendered all the more notable by the high position of the victim. The details were few and startling. A maidservant living alone in a house not far from the river, had gone upstairs to bed about eleven. Although a fog rolled over the city in the small hours, the early part of the night was cloudless, and the lane, which the maid's window overlooked, was brilliantly lit by the full moon. It seems she was romantically given; for she sat down upon her box, which stood immediately under the window, and fell into a dream of musing. Never (she used to say, with streaming tears, when she narrated that experience), never had she felt more at peace with all men or thought more

kindly of the world. And as she so sat she
became aware of an aged and beautiful
gentleman with white hair, drawing near
along the lane; and advancing to meet him,
another and very small gentleman, to whom
at first she paid less attention. When they
had come within speech (which was just
under the maid's eyes) the older man bowed
and accosted the other with a very pretty
manner of politeness. It did not seem as if
the subject of his address were of great importance; indeed, from his pointing, it sometimes appeared as if he were only inquiring
his way; but the moon shone on his face as
he spoke, and the girl was pleased to watch
it, it seemed to breathe such an innocent and
old-world kindness of disposition, yet with
something high too, as of a well-founded
self-content. Presently her eye wandered to
the other, and she was surprised to recognise
in him a certain Mr. Hyde, who had once
visited her master, and for whom she had
conceived a dislike. He had in his hand a
heavy cane, with which he was trifling; but

he answered never a word, and seemed to listen with an ill-contained impatience. And then all of a sudden he broke out in a great flame of anger, stamping with his foot, brandishing the cane, and carrying on (as the maid described it) like a madman. The old gentleman took a step back, with the air of one very much surprised and a trifle hurt; and at that Mr. Hyde broke out of all bounds, and clubbed him to the earth. And next moment, with ape-like fury, he was trampling his victim under foot, and hailing down a storm of blows, under which the bones were audibly shattered and the body jumped upon the roadway. At the horror of these sights and sounds, the maid fainted.

It was two o'clock when she came to herself and called for the police. The murderer was gone long ago; but there lay his victim in the middle of the lane, incredibly mangled. The stick with which the deed had been done, although it was of some rare and very tough and heavy wood, had broken in the middle under the stress of this insensate cruelty;

and one splintered half had rolled in the
neighbouring gutter—the other, without
doubt, had been carried away by the murderer.   A purse and a gold watch were found
upon the victim; but no cards or papers,
except a sealed and stamped envelope, which
he had been probably carrying to the post,
and which bore the name and address of
Mr. Utterson.

This was brought to the lawyer the next
morning, before he was out of bed; and he
had no sooner seen it, and been told the circumstances, than he shot out a solemn lip.
"I shall say nothing till I have seen the
body," said he; "this may be very serious.
Have the kindness to wait while I dress."
And with the same grave countenance he
hurried through his breakfast and drove to
the police station, whither the body had been
carried.   As soon as he came into the cell,
he nodded.

"Yes," said he, "I recognise him.   I am
sorry to say that this is Sir Danvers Carew."

"Good God, sir," exclaimed the officer, "is

it possible ? " And the next moment his eye lighted up with professional ambition. " This will make a deal of noise," he said. " And perhaps you can help us to the man." And he briefly narrated what the maid had seen, and showed the broken stick.

Mr. Utterson had already quailed at the name of Hyde ; but when the stick was laid before him, he could doubt no longer : broken and battered as it was, he recognised it for one that he had himself presented many years before to Henry Jekyll.

" Is this Mr. Hyde a person of small stature ? " he inquired.

" Particularly small and particularly wicked-looking, is what the maid calls him," said the officer.

Mr. Utterson reflected; and then, raising his head, " If you will come with me in my cab," he said, " I think I can take you to his house".

It was by this time about nine in the morning, and the first fog of the season. A great chocolate-coloured pall lowered over heaven, but the wind was continually charging

and routing these embattled vapours; so
that as the cab crawled from street to street,
Mr. Utterson beheld a marvellous number
of degrees and hues of twilight; for here it
would be dark like the back-end of evening;
and there would be a glow of a rich, lurid
brown, like the light of some strange conflagration; and here, for a moment, the fog
would be quite broken up, and a haggard
shaft of daylight would glance in between
the swirling wreaths. The dismal quarter
of Soho seen under these changing glimpses,
with its muddy ways, and slatternly passengers, and its lamps, which had never been
extinguished or had been kindled afresh to
combat this mournful reinvasion of darkness,
seemed, in the lawyer's eyes, like a district
of some city in a nightmare. The thoughts
of his mind, besides, were of the gloomiest
dye; and when he glanced at the companion
of his drive, he was conscious of some touch of
that terror of the law and the law's officers,
which may at times assail the most honest.

As the cab drew up before the address

indicated, the fog lifted a little and showed him a dingy street, a gin palace, a low French eating house, a shop for the retail of penny numbers and twopenny salads, many ragged children huddled in the doorways, and many women of many different nationalities passing out, key in hand, to have a morning glass; and the next moment the fog settled down again upon that part, as brown as umber, and cut him off from his blackguardly surroundings. This was the home of Henry Jekyll's favourite; of a man who was heir to a quarter of a million sterling.

An ivory-faced and silvery-haired old woman opened the door. She had an evil face, smoothed by hypocrisy; but her manners were excellent. Yes, she said, this was Mr. Hyde's, but he was not at home; he had been in that night very late, but had gone away again in less than an hour: there was nothing strange in that; his habits were very irregular, and he was often absent; for instance, it was nearly two months since she had seen him till yesterday.

"Very well then, we wish to see his rooms," said the lawyer; and when the woman began to declare it was impossible, "I had better tell you who this person is," he added. "This is Inspector Newcomen, of Scotland Yard."

A flash of odious joy appeared upon the woman's face. "Ah!" said she, "he is in trouble! What has he done?"

Mr. Utterson and the inspector exchanged glances. "He don't seem a very popular character," observed the latter. "And now, my good woman, just let me and this gentleman have a look about us."

In the whole extent of the house, which but for the old woman remained otherwise empty, Mr. Hyde had only used a couple of rooms; but these were furnished with luxury and good taste. A closet was filled with wine; the plate was of silver, the napery elegant; a good picture hung upon the walls, a gift (as Utterson supposed) from Henry Jekyll, who was much of a connoisseur; and the carpets were of many piles and agreeable in colour. At this moment, however, the rooms bore every mark of having been recently and hurriedly ransacked; clothes lay about the floor, with their pockets inside out; lockfast drawers stood open; and on the hearth there lay a pile of gray ashes, as though many papers had been burned. From these embers the inspector disinterred the butt end of a green cheque book, which had resisted the action of the fire; the other half of the stick was found behind the door; and as this clinched his suspicions, the officer declared himself delighted. A visit to the bank, where several thousand pounds were found to be lying to the murderer's credit, completed his gratification.

"You may depend upon it, sir," he told Mr. Utterson: "I have him in my hand. He must have lost his head, or he never would have left the stick, or, above all, burned the cheque book. Why, money's life to the man. We have nothing to do but wait for him at the bank, and get out the handbills."

This last, however, was not so easy of accomplishment ; for Mr. Hyde had numbered few familiars—even the master of the servant-maid had only seen him twice ; his family could nowhere be traced ; he had never been photographed ; and the few who could describe him differed widely, as common observers will.   Only on one point were they agreed ; and that was the haunting sense of unexpressed deformity with which the fugitive impressed his beholders.

INCIDENT OF THE LETTER.

IT was late in the afternoon, when Mr. Utterson found his way to Dr. Jekyll's door, where he was at once admitted by Poole, and carried down by the kitchen offices and across a yard which had once been a garden, to the building which was indifferently known as the laboratory or the dissecting rooms. The doctor had bought the house from the heirs of a celebrated surgeon; and his own tastes being rather chemical than anatomical, had changed the destination of the block at the bottom of the garden. It was the first time that the lawyer had been received in that part of his friend's quarters; and he eyed the dingy windowless structure with curiosity, and gazed round with a distasteful sense of strangeness as he crossed the theatre, once crowded with eager students and now lying gaunt and silent, the tables laden with chemical apparatus, the floor strewn with crates and littered with packing straw, and the light falling dimly through the foggy cupola. At the further end, a flight of stairs mounted to a door covered with red baize ; and through this, Mr. Utterson was at last received into the doctor's cabinet. It was a large room, fitted round with glass presses, furnished, among other things, with a cheval-glass and a business table, and looking out upon the court by three dusty windows barred with iron. The fire burned in the grate ; a lamp was set lighted on the chimney shelf, for even in the houses the fog began to lie thickly ; and there, close up to the warmth, sat Dr. Jekyll, looking deadly sick. He did not rise to meet his visitor, but held out a cold hand, and bade him welcome in a changed voice.

"And now," said Mr. Utterson, as soon as Poole had left them, " you have heard the news?"

The doctor shuddered. "They were crying it in the square," he said. "I heard them in my dining-room."

"One word," said the lawyer. "Carew was my client, but so are you; and I want to know what I am doing. You have not been mad enough to hide this fellow?"

"Utterson, I swear to God," cried the doctor, "I swear to God I will never set eyes on him again. I bind my honour to you that I am done with him in this world. It is all at an end. And indeed he does not want my help; you do not know him as I do; he is safe, he is quite safe; mark my words, he will never more be heard of."

The lawyer listened gloomily; he did not like his friend's feverish manner. "You seem pretty sure of him," said he; "and for your sake, I hope you may be right. If it came to a trial, your name might appear."

"I am quite sure of him," replied Jekyll; "I have grounds for certainty that I cannot share with any one. But there is one thing on which you may advise me. I have—I

have received a letter; and I am at a loss
whether I should show it to the police. I
should like to leave it in your hands,
Utterson; you would judge wisely, I am
sure; I have so great a trust in you."

"You fear, I suppose, that it might lead
to his detection?" asked the lawyer.

"No," said the other. "I cannot say that
I care what becomes of Hyde; I am quite
done with him. I was thinking of my own
character, which this hateful business has
rather exposed."

Utterson ruminated awhile; he was surprised at his friend's selfishness, and yet
relieved by it. "Well," said he, at last,
"let me see the letter."

The letter was written in an odd, upright
hand, and signed "Edward Hyde": and it
signified, briefly enough, that the writer's
benefactor, Dr. Jekyll, whom he had long so
unworthily repaid for a thousand generosities,
need labour under no alarm for his safety,
as he had means of escape on which he placed
a sure dependence   The lawyer liked this

letter well enough : it put a better colour on
the intimacy than he had looked for ; and
he blamed himself for some of his past
suspicions.

"Have you the envelope?" he asked.

"I burned it," replied Jekyll, "before I
thought what I was about.   But it bore no
postmark.   The note was handed in."

"Shall I keep this and sleep upon it?"
asked Utterson.

"I wish you to judge for me entirely,"
was the reply.   "I have lost confidence in
myself."

"Well, I shall consider," returned the
lawyer.   "And now one word more : it was
Hyde who dictated the terms in your will
about that disappearance?"

The doctor seemed seized with a qualm
of faintness ; he shut his mouth tight and
nodded.

"I knew it," said Utterson.   "He meant
to murder you.   You have had a fine escape."

"I have had what is far more to the
purpose," returned the doctor solemnly : "I

have had a lesson—O God, Utterson, what a lesson I have had!" And he covered his face for a moment with his hands.

On his way out, the lawyer stopped and had a word or two with Poole. "By the by," said he, "there was a letter handed in to-day: what was the messenger like?" But Poole was positive nothing had come except by post; "and only circulars by that," he added.

This news sent off the visitor with his fears renewed. Plainly the letter had come by the laboratory door; possibly, indeed, it had been written in the cabinet; and, if that were so, it must be differently judged, and handled with the more caution. The news-boys, as he went, were crying themselves hoarse along the footways: "Special edition. Shocking murder of an M.P." That was the funeral oration of one friend and client; and he could not help a certain apprehension lest the good name of another should be sucked down in the eddy of the scandal. It was, at least, a ticklish decision

that he had to make ; and, self-reliant as he
was by habit, he began to cherish a longing
for advice. It was not to be had directly ;
but perhaps, he thought, it might be fished
for.

Presently after, he sat on one side of his
own hearth, with Mr. Guest, his head clerk,
upon the other, and midway between, at a
nicely calculated distance from the fire, a
bottle of a particular old wine that had long
dwelt unsunned in the foundations of his
house. The fog still slept on the wing
above the drowned city, where the lamps
glimmered like-carbuncles ; and through the
muffle and smother of these fallen clouds, the
procession of the town's life was still rolling
in through the great arteries with a sound as
of a mighty wind. But the room was gay
with firelight. In the bottle the acids were
long ago resolved; the imperial dye had
softened with time, as the colour grows richer
in stained windows; and the glow of hot
autumn afternoons on hillside vineyards was
ready to be set free and to disperse the fogs

of London. Insensibly the lawyer melted. There was no man from whom he kept fewer secrets than Mr. Guest; and he was not always sure that he kept as many as he meant. Guest had often been on business to the doctor's: he knew Poole; he could scarce have failed to hear of Mr. Hyde's familiarity about the house; he might draw conclusions: was it not as well, then, that he should see a letter which put that mystery to rights? and, above all, since Guest, being a great student and critic of handwriting, would consider the step natural and obliging? The clerk, besides, was a man of counsel; he would scarce read so strange a document without dropping a remark; and by that remark Mr. Utterson might shape his future course.

"This is a sad business about Sir Danvers," he said.

"Yes, sir, indeed. It has elicited a great deal of public feeling," returned Guest. "The man, of course, was mad."

"I should like to hear your views on that,"

replied Utterson. "I have a document here in his handwriting; it is between ourselves, for I scarce know what to do about it; it is an ugly business at the best. But there it is; quite in your way: a murderer's autograph."

Guest's eyes brightened, and he sat down at once and studied it with passion. "No, sir," he said; "not mad; but it is an odd hand."

"And by all accounts a very odd writer," added the lawyer.

Just then the servant entered with a note.

"Is that from Dr. Jekyll, sir?" inquired the clerk. "I thought I knew the writing. Anything private, Mr. Utterson?"

"Only an invitation to dinner. Why? do you want to see it?"

"One moment. I thank you, sir;" and the clerk laid the two sheets of paper alongside and sedulously compared their contents. "Thank you, sir," he said at last, returning both; "it's a very interesting autograph."

There was a pause, during which Mr.

Utterson struggled with himself. "Why did you compare them, Guest?" he inquired suddenly.

"Well, sir," returned the clerk, "there's a rather singular resemblance; the two hands are in many points identical: only differently sloped."

"Rather quaint," said Utterson.

"It is, as you say, rather quaint," returned Guest.

"I wouldn't speak of this note, you know," said the master.

"No, sir," said the clerk. "I understand."

But no sooner was Mr. Utterson alone that night, than he locked the note into his safe, where it reposed from that time forward. "What!" he thought. "Henry Jekyll forge for a murderer!" And his blood ran cold in his veins.

REMARKABLE INCIDENT OF DR. LANYON.

TIME ran on; thousands of pounds were offered in reward, for the death of Sir Danvers was resented as a public injury; but Mr. Hyde had disappeared out of the ken of the police as though he had never existed. Much of his past was unearthed, indeed, and all disreputable: tales came out of the man's cruelty, at once so callous and violent, of his vile life, of his strange associates, of the hatred that seemed to have surrounded his career; but of his present whereabouts, not a whisper. From the time he had left the house in Soho on the morning of the murder, he was simply blotted out; and gradually, as time drew on, Mr. Utterson began to recover from the hotness of his alarm, and to grow more at quiet with himself. The death of Sir Danvers was, to his way of thinking, more than paid for by the disappearance of Mr. Hyde. Now that that evil influence had been withdrawn, a new life began for Dr. Jekyll. He came out of his seclusion, renewed relations with his friends, became once more their familiar guest and entertainer; and whilst he had always been known for charities, he was now no less distinguished for religion. He was busy, he was much in the open air, he did good; his face seemed to open and brighten, as if with an inward consciousness of service; and for more than two months, the doctor was at peace.

On the 8th of January Utterson had dined at the doctor's with a small party; Lanyon had been there; and the face of the host had looked from one to the other as in the old days when the trio were inseparable friends. On the 12th, and again on the 14th, the door was shut against the lawyer. "The doctor was confined to the house," Poole said, "and saw no one." On the

15th, he tried again, and was again refused; and having now been used for the last two months to see his friend almost daily, he found this return of solitude to weigh upon his spirits. The fifth night, he had in Guest to dine with him; and the sixth he betook himself to Dr. Lanyon's.

There at least he was not denied admittance; but when he came in, he was shocked at the change which had taken place in the doctor's appearance. He had his death-warrant written legibly upon his face. The rosy man had grown pale; his flesh had fallen away; he was visibly balder and older; and yet it was not so much these tokens of a swift physical decay that arrested the lawyer's notice, as a look in the eye and quality of manner that seemed to testify to some deep-seated terror of the mind. It was unlikely that the doctor should fear death; and yet that was what Utterson was tempted to suspect. "Yes," he thought; "he is a doctor, he must know his own state and that his days are counted; and the knowledge is more than he can bear." And yet when Utterson remarked on his ill looks, it was with an air of great firmness that Lanyon declared himself a doomed man.

"I have had a shock," he said, "and I shall never recover. It is a question of weeks. Well, life has been pleasant; I liked it; yes, sir, I used to like it. I sometimes think if we knew all, we should be more glad to get away."

"Jekyll is ill, too," observed Utterson. "Have you seen him?"

But Lanyon's face changed, and he held up a trembling hand. "I wish to see or hear no more of Dr. Jekyll," he said, in a loud, unsteady voice. "I am quite done with that person; and I beg that you will spare me any allusion to one whom I regard as dead."

"Tut, tut!" said Mr. Utterson; and then, after a considerable pause, "Can't I do anything?" he inquired. "We are three very old friends, Lanyon; we shall not live to make others."

"Nothing can be done," returned Lanyon; "ask himself."

"He will not see me," said the lawyer.

"I am not surprised at that," was the reply. "Some day, Utterson, after I am dead, you may perhaps come to learn the right and wrong of this. I cannot tell you. And in the meantime, if you can sit and talk with me of other things, for God's sake, stay and do so; but if you cannot keep clear of this accursed topic, then, in God's name, go, for I cannot bear it."

As soon as he got home, Utterson sat down and wrote to Jekyll, complaining of his exclusion from the house, and asking the cause of this unhappy break with Lanyon; and the next day brought him a long answer, often very pathetically worded, and sometimes darkly mysterious in drift. The quarrel with Lanyon was incurable. "I do not blame our old friend," Jekyll wrote, "but I share his view that we must never meet. I mean from henceforth to lead a life of extreme seclusion; you must not be surprised, nor must you doubt my friendship, if my door is often shut even to you. You must suffer me to go my own dark way. I have brought on myself a punishment and a danger that I cannot name. If I am the chief of sinners, I am the chief of sufferers also. I could not think that this earth contained a place for sufferings and terrors so unmanning; and you can do but one thing, Utterson, to lighten this destiny, and that is to respect my silence." Utterson was amazed; the dark influence of Hyde had been withdrawn, the doctor had returned to his old tasks and amities; a week ago, the prospect had smiled with every promise of a cheerful and an honoured age; and now in a moment, friendship and peace of mind and the whole tenor of his life were wrecked. So great and unprepared a change pointed to madness; but in view of Lanyon's manner and words, there must lie for it some deeper ground.

A week afterwards Dr. Lanyon took to

his bed, and in something less than a fort-night he was dead. The night after the funeral, at which he had been sadly affected, Utterson locked the door of his business room, and sitting there by the light of a melancholy candle, drew out and set before him an envelope addressed by the hand and sealed with the seal of his dead friend. "PRIVATE : for the hands of J. G. Utterson ALONE, and in case of his predecease *to be destroyed unread*," so it was emphatically superscribed ; and the lawyer dreaded to behold the contents. "I have buried one friend to-day," he thought : "what if this should cost me another?" And then he condemned the fear as a disloyalty, and broke the seal. Within there was another enclosure, likewise sealed, and marked upon the cover as "not to be opened till the death or disappearance of Dr. Henry Jekyll". Utterson could not trust his eyes. Yes, it was disappearance ; here again, as in the mad will, which he had long ago restored to its author, here again were the idea of a disappearance and the name of Henry Jekyll bracketed. But in the will, that idea had sprung from the sinister suggestion of the man Hyde; it was set there with a purpose all too plain and horrible. Written by the hand of Lanyon, what should it mean? A great curiosity came to the trustee, to disregard the prohibition, and dive at once to the bottom of these mysteries; but professional honour and faith to his dead friend were stringent obligations; and the packet slept in the inmost corner of his private safe.

It is one thing to mortify curiosity, another to conquer it; and it may be doubted if, from that day forth, Utterson desired the society of his surviving friend with the same eagerness. He thought of him kindly; but his thoughts were disquieted and fearful. He went to call indeed; but he was perhaps relieved to be denied admittance; perhaps, in his heart, he preferred to speak with Poole upon the doorstep, and surrounded by the air and sounds of the open city, rather than to be admitted into that house of voluntary bondage, and to sit and speak with its inscrutable recluse. Poole had, indeed, no very pleasant news to communicate. The doctor, it appeared, now more than ever confined himself to the cabinet over the laboratory, where he would sometimes even sleep : he was out of spirits, he had grown very silent, he did not read ; it seemed as if he had something on his mind. Utterson became so used to the unvarying character of these reports, that he fell off little by little in the frequency of his visits.

INCIDENT AT THE WINDOW.

IT chanced on Sunday, when Mr. Utterson was on his usual walk with Mr. Enfield, that their way lay once again through the by-street; and that when they came in front of the door, both stopped to gaze on it.

"Well," said Enfield, "that story's at an end, at least. We shall never see more of Mr. Hyde."

"I hope not," said Utterson. "Did I ever tell you that I once saw him, and shared your feeling of repulsion?"

"It was impossible to do the one without the other," returned Enfield. "And, by the way, what an ass you must have thought me, not to know that this was a back way to Dr. Jekyll's! It was partly your own fault that I found it out, even when I did."

"So you found it out, did you?" said Utterson. "But if that be so, we may step into the court and take a look at the windows. To tell you the truth, I am uneasy about poor Jekyll; and even outside, I feel as if the presence of a friend might do him good."

The court was very cool and a little damp, and full of premature twilight, although the sky, high up overhead, was still bright with sunset. The middle one of the three windows was half way open; and sitting close beside it, taking the air with an infinite sadness of mien, like some disconsolate prisoner, Utterson saw Dr. Jekyll.

"What! Jekyll!" he cried. "I trust you are better."

"I am very low, Utterson," replied the doctor drearily; "very low. It will not last long, thank God."

"You stay too much indoors," said the lawyer. "You should be out, whipping up the circulation, like Mr. Enfield and me.

(This is my cousin — Mr. Enfield — Dr. Jekyll) Come now; get your hat, and take a quick turn with us."

"You are very good," sighed the other. "I should like to very much; but no, no, no; it is quite impossible; I dare not. But indeed, Utterson, I am very glad to see you; this is really a great pleasure. I would ask you and Mr. Enfield up, but the place is really not fit."

"Why then," said the lawyer, good-naturedly, "the best thing we can do is to stay down here, and speak with you from where we are."

"That is just what I was about to venture to propose," returned the doctor, with a smile. But the words were hardly uttered, before the smile was struck out of his face and succeeded by an expression of such abject terror and despair, as froze the very blood of the two gentlemen below. They saw It but for a glimpse, for the window was instantly thrust down; but that glimpse had been sufficient, and they turned and left the court without a word. In silence, too, they traversed the by-street; and it was not until they had come into a neighbouring thorough-fare, where even upon a Sunday there were still some stirrings of life, that Mr. Utterson at last turned and looked at his companion. They were both pale; and there was an answering horror in their eyes.

"God forgive us! God forgive us!" said Mr. Utterson.

But Mr. Enfield only nodded his head very seriously, and walked on once more in silence.

THE LAST NIGHT.

MR. UTTERSON was sitting by his fireside
one evening after dinner, when he was
surprised to receive a visit from Poole.

" Bless me, Poole, what brings you here?"
he cried; and then, taking a second look at
him, "What ails you?" he added; "is the
doctor ill?"

" Mr Utterson," said the man, "there is
something wrong."

" Take a seat, and here is a glass of wine
for you," said the lawyer. " Now, take
your time, and tell me plainly what you
want."

" You know the doctor's ways, sir," replied Poole, " and how he shuts himself up.
Well, he's shut up again in the cabinet; and
I don't like it, sir—I wish I may die if I
like it. Mr. Utterson, sir, I'm afraid."

" Now, my good man," said the lawyer, " be explicit. What are you afraid of?"

" I've been afraid for about a week," returned Poole, doggedly disregarding the question; "and I can bear it no more."

The man's appearance amply bore out his words; his manner was altered for the worse: and except for the moment when he had first announced his terror, he had not once looked the lawyer in the face. Even now, he sat with the glass of wine untasted on his knee, and his eyes directed to a corner of the floor. " I can bear it no more," he repeated.

" Come," said the lawyer, " I see you have some good reason, Poole; I see there is something seriously amiss. Try to tell me what it is."

" I think there's been foul play," said Poole, hoarsely.

" Foul play!" cried the lawyer, a good deal frightened, and rather inclined to be irritated in consequence. " What foul play? What does the man mean?"

"I daren't say, sir," was the answer;
"but will you come along with me and see
for yourself?"

Mr. Utterson's only answer was to rise
and get his hat and great coat; but he
observed with wonder the greatness of the
relief that appeared upon the butler's face,
and perhaps with no less, that the wine was
still untasted when he set it down to follow.

It was a wild, cold, seasonable night of
March, with a pale moon, lying on her back
as though the wind had tilted her, and a
flying wrack of the most diaphanous and
lawny texture. The wind made talking
difficult, and flecked the blood into the face.
It seemed to have swept the streets un-
usually bare of passengers, besides; for Mr.
Utterson thought he had never seen that
part of London so deserted. He could have
wished it otherwise; never in his life had he
been conscious of so sharp a wish to see and
touch his fellow-creatures; for, struggle as
he might, there was borne in upon his mind
a crushing anticipation of calamity. The

square, when they got there, was all full of wind and dust, and the thin trees in the garden were lashing themselves along the railing. Poole, who had kept all the way a. pace or two ahead, now pulled up in the middle of the pavement, and in spite of the biting weather, took off his hat and mopped his brow with a red pocket-handkerchief. But for all the hurry of his coming, these were not the dews of exertion that he wiped away, but the moisture of some strangling anguish; for his face was white, and his voice, when he spoke, harsh and broken.

"Well, sir," he said, "here we are, and God grant there be nothing wrong."

"Amen, Poole," said the lawyer.

Thereupon the servant knocked in a very guarded manner; the door was opened on the chain; and a voice asked from within, "Is that you, Poole?"

"It's all right," said Poole. "Open the door."

The hall, when they entered it, was brightly lighted up; the fire was built high;

and about the hearth the whole of the servants, men and women, stood huddled together like a flock of sheep. At the sight of Mr. Utterson, the housemaid broke into hysterical whimpering ; and the cook, crying out, " Bless God ! it's Mr. Utterson," ran forward as if to take him in her arms.

" What, what ? Are you all here ? " said the lawyer, peevishly. " Very irregular, very unseemly ; your master would be far from pleased."

" They're all afraid," said Poole.

Blank silence followed, no one protesting ; only the maid lifted up her voice, and now wept loudly.

" Hold your tongue ! " Poole said to her, with a ferocity of accent that testified to his own jangled nerves ; and indeed when the girl had so suddenly raised the note of her lamentation, they had all started and turned towards the inner door with faces of dreadful expectation. " And now," continued the butler, addressing the knife-boy, " reach me a candle, and we'll get this through hands

at once." And then he begged Mr. Utter
son to follow him, and led the way to the
back garden.

"Now, sir," said he, "you come as gently
as you can. I want you to hear, and I don't
want you to be heard. And see here, sir, if
by any chance he was to ask you in, don't
go."

Mr. Utterson's nerves, at this unlooked-
for termination, gave a jerk that nearly
threw him from his balance; but he re-col-
lected his courage, and followed the butler
into the laboratory building and through the
surgical theatre, with its lumber of crates
and bottles, to the foot of the stair. Here
Poole motioned him to stand on one side
and listen; while he himself, setting down
the candle and making a great and obvious
call on his resolution, mounted the steps, and
knocked with a somewhat uncertain hand on
the red baize of the cabinet door.

"Mr. Utterson, sir, asking to see you,"
he called; and even as he did so, once more
violently signed to the lawyer to give ear.

A voice answered from within: "Tell him I cannot see any one," it said, complainingly.

"Thank you, sir," said Poole, with a note of something like triumph in his voice; and taking up his candle, he led Mr. Utterson back across the yard and into the great kitchen, where the fire was out and the beetles were leaping on the floor.

"Sir," he said, looking Mr. Utterson in the eyes, "was that my master's voice?"

"It seems much changed," replied the lawyer, very pale, but giving look for look.

"Changed? Well, yes, I think so," said the butler. "Have I been twenty years in this man's house, to be deceived about his voice? No, sir; master's made away with; he was made away with, eight days ago, when we heard him cry out upon the name of God; and *who's* in there instead of him, and *why* it stays there, is a thing that cries to Heaven, Mr. Utterson!"

"This is a very strange tale, Poole; this is rather a wild tale, my man," said Mr.

Utterson, biting his finger. "Suppose it were as you suppose, supposing Dr. Jekyll to have been—well, murdered, what could induce the murderer to stay? That won't hold water; it doesn't commend itself to reason."

"Well, Mr. Utterson, you are a hard man to satisfy, but I'll do it yet," said Poole. "All this last week (you must know) him, or it, or whatever it is that lives in that cabinet, has been crying night and day for some sort of medicine and cannot get it to his mind. It was sometimes his way—the master's, that is—to write his orders on a sheet of paper and throw it on the stair. We've had nothing else this week back; nothing but papers, and a closed door, and the very meals left there to be smuggled in when nobody was looking. Well, sir, every day, ay, and twice and thrice in the same day, there have been orders and complaints, and I have been sent flying to all the wholesale chemists in town. Every time I brought the stuff back, there would be another paper telling me to return it, because it was not

pure, and another order to a different firm.
This drug is wanted bitter bad, sir, whatever
for."

" Have you any of these papers?" asked
Mr. Utterson.

Poole felt in his pocket and handed out a
crumpled note, which the lawyer, bending
nearer to the candle, carefully examined.
Its contents ran thus: " Dr. Jekyll presents
his compliments to Messrs. Maw. He as-
sures them that their last sample is impure
and quite useless for his present purpose.
In the year 18—, Dr. J. purchased a somewhat large quantity from Messrs. M. He
now begs them to search with the most
sedulous care, and should any of the
same quality be left, to forward it to him at
once. Expense is no consideration. The
importance of this to Dr. J. can hardly be
exaggerated." So far the letter had run
composedly enough ; but here, with a sudden
splutter of the pen, the writer's emotion had
broken loose. " For God's sake," he had
added, "find me some of the old."

" This is a strange note," said Mr. Utterson ; and then, sharply, " How do you come to have it open?"

" The man at Maw's was main angry, sir, and he threw it back to me like so much dirt," returned Poole.

" This is unquestionably the doctor's hand, do you know?" resumed the lawyer.

" I thought it looked like it," said the servant, rather sulkily ; and then, with another voice, " But what matters hand of write?" he said. " I've seen him!"

" Seen him?" repeated Mr. Utterson. "Well?"

" That's it!" said Poole. " It was this way. I came suddenly into the theatre from the garden. It seems he had slipped out to look for this drug, or whatever it is ; for the cabinet door was open, and there he was at the far end of the room, digging among the crates. He looked up when I came in, gave a kind of cry, and whipped upstairs into the cabinet. It was but for one minute that I saw him, but the hair stood upon my head like quills. Sir, if that was my master, why had he a mask upon his face? If it was my master, why did he cry out like a rat, and run from me? I have served him long enough. And then . . ." the man paused, and passed his hand over his face.

"These are all very strange circumstances," said Mr. Utterson, "but I think I begin to see daylight. Your master, Poole, is plainly seized with one of those maladies that both torture and deform the sufferer; hence, for aught I know, the alteration of his voice; hence the mask and his avoidance of his friends; hence his eagerness to find this drug, by means of which the poor soul retains some hope of ultimate recovery—God grant that he be not deceived! There is my explanation; it is sad enough, Poole, ay, and appalling to consider; but it is plain and natural, hangs well together, and delivers us from all exorbitant alarms."

"Sir," said the butler, turning to a sort of mottled pallor, "that thing was not my

master, and there's the truth. My master"
—here he looked round him, and began to
whisper—" is a tall fine build of a man, and
this was more of a dwarf." Utterson attempted to protest. "O, sir," cried Poole,
" do you think I do not know my master after
twenty years? do you think I do not know
where his head comes to in the cabinet door,
where I saw him every morning of my life?
No, sir, that thing in the mask was never
Dr. Jekyll—God knows what it was, but
it was never Dr. Jekyll; and it is the
belief of my heart that there was murder
done."

"Poole," replied the lawyer, "if you say
that, it will become my duty to make certain.
Much as I desire to spare your master's
feelings, much as I am puzzled by this note,
which seems to prove him to be still alive,
I shall consider it my duty to break in that
door."

" Ah, Mr. Utterson, that's talking!" cried
the butler.

"And now comes the second question,"

6

resumed Utterson: "Who is going to do it?"

"Why, you and me, sir," was the undaunted reply.

"That is very well said," returned the lawyer; "and whatever comes of it, I shall make it my business to see you are no loser."

"There is an axe in the theatre," continued Poole; "and you might take the kitchen poker for yourself."

The lawyer took that rude but weighty instrument into his hand, and balanced it. "Do you know, Poole," he said, looking up, "that you and I are about to place ourselves in a position of some peril?"

"You may say so, sir, indeed," returned the butler.

"It is well, then, that we should be frank," said the other. "We both think more than we have said; let us make a clean breast. This masked figure that you saw, did you recognise it?"

"Well, sir, it went so quick, and the

creature was so doubled up, that I could hardly swear to that," was the answer. " But if you mean, was it Mr. Hyde?—why, yes, I think it was! You see, it was much of the same bigness; and it had the same quick light way with it; and then who else could have got in by the laboratory door? You have not forgot, sir, that at the time of the murder he had still the key with him? But that's not all. I don't know, Mr Utterson, if ever you met this Mr. Hyde?"

"Yes," said the lawyer, " I once spoke with him."

" Then you must know, as well as the rest of us, that there was something queer about that gentleman—something that gave a man a turn—I don't know rightly how to say it, sir, beyond this : that you felt it in your marrow—kind of cold and thin."

"I own I felt something of what you describe," said Mr. Utterson.

"Quite so, sir," returned Poole. "Well, when that masked thing like a monkey jumped from among the chemicals and

whipped into the cabinet, it went down my
spine like ice.   O, I know it's not evidence,
Mr. Utterson; I'm book-learned enough for
that; but a man has his feelings; and I give
you my bible-word it was Mr. Hyde!"

"Ay, ay," said the lawyer.   "My fears
incline to the same point.   Evil, I fear,
founded—evil was sure to come—of that
connection.   Ay, truly, I believe you; I
believe poor Harry is killed; and I believe
his murderer (for what purpose, God alone
can tell) is still lurking in his victim's room.
Well, let our name be vengeance.   Call
Bradshaw."

The footman came at the summons, very
white and nervous.

"Pull yourself together, Bradshaw," said
the lawyer.   "This suspense, I know, is
telling upon all of you; but it is now our
intention to make an end of it.   Poole, here,
and I are going to force our way into the
cabinet.   If all is well, my shoulders are
broad enough to bear the blame.   Meanwhile, lest anything should really be amiss,

or any malefactor seek to escape by the
back, you and the boy must go round the
corner with a pair of good sticks, and take
your post at the laboratory door. We give
you ten minutes to get to your stations."

As Bradshaw left, the lawyer looked at
his watch. "And now, Poole, let us get
to ours," he said; and taking the poker
under his arm, he led the way into the yard.
The scud had banked over the moon, and
it was now quite dark. The wind, which
only broke in puffs and draughts into that
deep well of building, tossed the light of the
candle to and fro about their steps, until
they came into the shelter of the theatre,
where they sat down silently to wait.
London hummed solemnly all around; but
nearer at hand, the stillness was only broken
by the sound of a footfall moving to and fro
along the cabinet floor.

"So it will walk all day, sir," whispered
Poole; "ay, and the better part of the night.
Only when a new sample comes from the
chemist, there's a bit of a break. Ah, it's an

ill conscience that's such an enemy to rest! Ah, sir, there's blood foully shed in every step of it! But hark again, a little closer— put your heart in your ears, Mr. Utterson, and tell me, is that the doctor's foot?"

The steps fell lightly and oddly, with a certain swing, for all they went so slowly; it was different indeed from the heavy creaking tread of Henry Jekyll. Utterson sighed. "Is there never anything else?" he asked.

Poole nodded. "Once," he said. "Once I heard it weeping!"

"Weeping? how that?" said the lawyer, conscious of a sudden chill of horror.

"Weeping like a woman or a lost soul," said the butler. "I came away with that upon my heart, that I could have wept too."

But now the ten minutes drew to an end. Poole disinterred the axe from under a stack of packing straw; the candle was set upon the nearest table to light them to the attack; and they drew near with bated breath to where that patient foot was still going up and down, up and down in the quiet of the night.

"Jekyll," cried Utterson, with a loud voice, "I demand to see you." He paused a moment, but there came no reply. "I give you fair warning, our suspicions are aroused, and I must and shall see you," he resumed; "if not by fair means, then by foul—if not of your consent, then by brute force!"

"Utterson," said the voice, "for God's sake, have mercy!"

"Ah, that's not Jekyll's voice—it's Hyde's!" cried Utterson. "Down with the door, Poole!"

Poole swung the axe over his shoulder; the blow shook the building, and the red baize door leaped against the lock and hinges. A dismal screech, as of mere animal terror, rang from the cabinet. Up went the axe again, and again the panels crashed and the frame bounded; four times the blow fell; but the wood was tough and the fittings were of excellent workmanship; and it was not until the fifth, that the lock burst in sunder, and the wreck of the door fell inwards on the carpet.

The besiegers, appalled by their own riot and the stillness that had succeeded, stood back a little and peered in. There lay the cabinet before their eyes in the quiet lamp-light, a good fire glowing and chattering on the hearth, the kettle singing its thin strain, a drawer or two open, papers neatly set forth on the business table, and nearer the fire, the things laid out for tea: the quietest room, you would have said, and, but for the glazed presses full of chemicals, the most commonplace that night in London.

Right in the midst there lay the body of a man sorely contorted and still twitching. They drew near on tiptoe, turned it on his back, and beheld the face of Edward Hyde. He was dressed in clothes far too large for him, clothes of the doctor's bigness; the cords of his face still moved with a semblance of life, but life was quite gone; and by the crushed phial in the hand and the strong smell of kernels that hung upon the air, Utterson knew that he was looking on the body of a self-destroyer.

"We have come too late," he said sternly, "whether to save or punish. Hyde is gone to his account; and it only remains for us to find the body of your master."

The far greater proportion of the building was occupied by the theatre, which filled almost the whole ground storey, and was lighted from above, and by the cabinet, which formed an upper storey at one end and looked upon the court. A corridor joined the theatre to the door on the by-street; and with this, the cabinet communicated separately by a second flight of stairs. There were besides a few dark closets and a spacious cellar. All these they now thoroughly examined. Each closet needed but a glance, for all were empty, and all, by the dust that fell from their doors, had stood long unopened.

The cellar, indeed, was filled with crazy lumber, mostly dating from the times of the surgeon who was Jekyll's predecessor; but even as they opened the door, they were advertised of the uselessness of further search, by the fall of a perfect mat of cob-web which had for years sealed up the entrance. Nowhere was there any trace of Henry Jekyll, dead or alive.

Poole stamped on the flags of the corridor. "He must be buried here," he said, hearkening to the sound.

"Or he may have fled," said Utterson, and he turned to examine the door in the by-street. It was locked; and lying near by on the flags, they found the key, already stained with rust.

"This does not look like use," observed the lawyer.

"Use!" echoed Poole. "Do you not see, sir, it is broken? much as if a man had stamped on it."

"Ah," continued Utterson, "and the fractures, too, are rusty." The two men looked at each other with a scare. "This is beyond me, Poole," said the lawyer. "Let us go back to the cabinet."

They mounted the stair in silence, and still, with an occasional awestruck glance at the dead body, proceeded more thoroughly to examine the contents of the cabinet. At one table, there were traces of chemical work, various measured heaps of some white salt being laid on glass saucers, as though for an experiment in which the unhappy man had been prevented.

"That is the same drug that I was always bringing him," said Poole; and even as he spoke, the kettle with a startling noise boiled over.

This brought them to the fireside, where the easy chair was drawn cosily up, and the tea things stood ready to the sitter's elbow, the very sugar in the cup. There were several books on a shelf; one lay beside the tea things open, and Utterson was amazed to find it a copy of a pious work, for which Jekyll had several times expressed a great esteem, annotated, in his own hand, with startling blasphemies.

Next, in the course of their review of the chamber, the searchers came to the cheval glass, into whose depth they looked with an involuntary horror. But it was so turned as to show them nothing but the rosy glow playing on the roof, the fire sparkling in a hundred repetitions along the glazed front of the presses, and their own pale and fearful countenances stooping to look in.

"This glass has seen some strange things, sir," whispered Poole.

"And surely none stranger than itself," echoed the lawyer, in the same tone. "For what did Jekyll "—he caught himself up at the word with a start, and then conquering the weakness : "what could Jekyll want with it?" he said.

"You may say that!" said Poole.

Next they turned to the business table. On the desk among the neat array of papers, a large envelope was uppermost, and bore, in the doctor's hand, the name of Mr. Utterson.

The lawyer unsealed it, and several enclosures fell to the floor. The first was a will, drawn in the same eccentric terms as the one which he had returned six months before, to serve as a testament in case of death and as a deed of gift in case of disappearance; but in place of the name of Edward Hyde, the lawyer, with indescribable amazement, read the name of Gabriel John Utterson. He looked at Poole, and then back at the papers, and last of all at the dead malefactor stretched upon the carpet.

"My head goes round," he said. "He has been all these days in possession; he had no cause to like me; he must have raged to see himself displaced; and he has not destroyed this document."

He caught the next paper; it was a brief note in the doctor's hand, and dated at the top. "O Poole!" the lawyer cried, "he was alive and here this day. He cannot have been disposed of in so short a space; he must be still alive, he must have fled! And then, why fled? and how? and in that case can we venture to declare this suicide? O, we must be careful. I foresee that we may yet involve your master in some dire catastrophe."

"Why don't you read it, sir?" asked Poole.

"Because I fear," replied the lawyer, solemnly. "God grant I have no cause for it!" And with that he brought the paper to his eye, and read as follows:—

"My dear Utterson,—When this shall fall into your hands, I shall have disappeared, under what circumstances I have not the penetration to foresee; but my instincts and all the circumstances of my nameless situation tell me that the end is sure and must be early. Go then, and first read the narrative which Lanyon warned me he was to place in your hands; and if you care to hear more, turn to the confession of

"Your unworthy and unhappy friend,

"HENRY JEKYLL."

"There was a third enclosure?" asked Utterson.

"Here, sir," said Poole, and gave into his hands a considerable packet sealed in several places.

The lawyer put it in his pocket. "I would say nothing of this paper. If your master has fled or is dead, we may at least save his credit. It is now ten; I must go home and read these documents in quiet; but I shall be back before midnight, when we shall send for the police."

They went out, locking the door of the theatre behind them; and Utterson, once more leaving the servants gathered about the fire in the hall, trudged back to his office to read the two narratives in which this mystery was now to be explained.

DR. LANYON'S NARRATIVE.

ON the ninth of January, now four days ago, I received by the evening delivery a registered envelope, addressed in the hand of my colleague and old school-companion, Henry Jekyll. I was a good deal surprised by this; for we were by no means in the habit of correspondence; I had seen the man, dined with him, indeed, the night before; and I could imagine nothing in our intercourse that should justify the formality of registration. The contents increased my wonder; for this is how the letter ran:—

"*10th December*, 18—

"Dear Lanyon,—You are one of my oldest friends; and although we may have differed at times on scientific questions, I cannot remember, at least on my side, any break in our affection. There was never a

day when, if you had said to me, 'Jekyll,
my life, my honour, my reason, depend upon
you,' I would not have sacrificed my fortune
or my left hand to help you. Lanyon, my
life, my honour, my reason, are all at your
mercy; if you fail me to-night, I am lost.
You might suppose, after this preface, that I
am going to ask you for something dis-
honourable to grant. Judge for yourself.

" I want you to postpone all other engage-
ments for to-night—ay, even if you were
summoned to the bedside of an emperor; to
take a cab, unless your carriage should be
actually at the door; and, with this letter in
your hand for consultation, to drive straight
to my house. Poole, my butler, has his
orders; you will find him waiting your
arrival with a locksmith. The door of my
cabinet is then to be forced; and you are to
go in alone; to open the glazed press (letter
E) on the left hand, breaking the lock if it
be shut; and to draw out, *with all its
contents as they stand*, the fourth drawer from
the top or (which is the same thing) the

third from the bottom. In my extreme distress of mind, I have a morbid fear of misdirecting you ; but even if I am in error, you may know the right drawer by its contents: some powders, a phial, and a paper book. This drawer I beg of you to carry back with you to Cavendish Square exactly as it stands.

" That is the first part of the service : now for the second. You should be back, if you set out at once on the receipt of this, long before midnight ; but I will leave you that amount of margin, not only in the fear of one of those obstacles that can neither be prevented nor foreseen, but because an hour when your servants are in bed is to be preferred for what will then remain to do. At midnight, then, I have to ask you to be alone in your consulting room, to admit with your own hand into the house a man who will present himself in my name, and to place in his hands the drawer that you will have brought with you from my cabinet. Then you will have played your part, and earned my gratitude completely. Five minutes afterwards, if you insist upon an explanation, you will have understood that these arrangements are of capital import- ance; and that by the neglect of one of them, fantastic as they must appear, you might have charged your conscience with my death or the shipwreck of my reason.

" Confident as I am that you will not trifle with this appeal, my heart sinks and my hand trembles at the bare thought of such a possibility. Think of me at this hour, in a strange place, labouring under a blackness of distress that no fancy can exaggerate, and yet well aware that, if you will but punctu- ally serve me, my troubles will roll away like a story that is told. Serve me, my dear Lanyon, and save

" Your friend,

" H. J.

" P.S.—I had already sealed this up when a fresh terror struck upon my soul. It is possible that the post office may fail me, and this letter not come into your hands until to-

morrow morning. In that case, dear Lanyon,
do my errand when it shall be most con-
venient for you in the course of the day ; and
once more expect my messenger at midnight. It may then already be too late ; and
if that night passes without event, you will
know that you have seen the last of Henry
Jekyll."

Upon the reading of this letter, I made
sure my colleague was insane ; but till that
was proved beyond the possibility of doubt,
I felt bound to do as he requested. The
less I understood of this farrago, the less I
was in a position to judge of its importance ;
and an appeal so worded could not be set
aside without a grave responsibility. I rose
accordingly from table, got into a hansom,
and drove straight to Jekyll's house. The
butler was awaiting my arrival ; he had received by the same post as mine a registered
letter of instruction, and had sent at once for
a locksmith and a carpenter. The trades-
men came while we were yet speaking ; and

we moved in a body to old Dr. Denman's surgical theatre, from which (as you are doubtless aware) Jekyll's private cabinet is most conveniently entered. The door was very strong, the lock excellent; the carpenter avowed he would have great trouble, and have to do much damage, if force were to be used; and the locksmith was near despair. But this last was a handy fellow, and after two hours' work, the door stood open. The press marked E was unlocked; and I took out the drawer, had it filled up with straw and tied in a sheet, and returned with it to Cavendish Square.

Here I proceeded to examine its contents. The powders were neatly enough made up, but not with the nicety of the dispensing chemist; so that it was plain they were of Jekyll's private manufacture; and when I opened one of the wrappers, I found what seemed to me a simple crystalline salt of a white colour. The phial, to which I next turned my attention, might have been about half full of a blood-red liquor, which was

highly pungent to the sense of smell, and
seemed to me to contain phosphorus and
some volatile ether. At the other ingredi-
ents I could make no guess. The book was
an ordinary version book, and contained little
but a series of dates. These covered a
period of many years; but I observed that
the entries ceased nearly a year ago, and
quite abruptly. Here and there a brief remark
was appended to a date, usually no more
than a single word: "double" occurring
perhaps six times in a total of several
hundred entries; and once very early in the
list, and followed by several marks of ex-
clamation, "total failure!!!" All this,
though it whetted my curiosity, told me little
that was definite. Here were a phial of
some tincture, a paper of some salt, and the
record of a series of experiments that had led
(like too many of Jekyll's investigations) to
no end of practical usefulness. How could
the presence of these articles in my house
affect either the honour, the sanity, or the
life of my flighty colleague? If his messenger

could go to one place, why could he not go to another? And even granting some impediment, why was this gentleman to be received by me in secret? The more I reflected, the more convinced I grew that I was dealing with a case of cerebral disease; and though I dismissed my servants to bed, I loaded an old revolver, that I might be found in some posture of self-defence.

Twelve o'clock had scarce rung out over London, ere the knocker sounded very gently on the door. I went myself at the summons, and found a small man crouching against the pillars of the portico.

"Are you come from Dr. Jekyll?" I asked.

He told me "yes" by a constrained gesture; and when I had bidden him enter, he did not obey me without a searching backward glance into the darkness of the square. There was a policeman not far off, advancing with his bull's eye open; and at the sight, I thought my visitor started and made greater haste.

These particulars struck me, I confess, disagreeably; and as I followed him into the bright light of the consulting room, I kept my hand ready on my weapon. Here, at last, I had a chance of clearly seeing him. I had never set eyes on him before, so much was certain. He was small, as I have said; I was struck besides with the shocking expression of his face, with his remarkable combination of great muscular activity and great apparent debility of constitution, and —last but not least—with the odd, subjective disturbance caused by his neighbourhood. This bore some resemblance to incipient rigor, and was accompanied by a marked sinking of the pulse. At the time, I set it down to some idiosyncratic, personal distaste, and merely wondered at the acuteness of the symptoms; but I have since had reason to believe the cause to lie much deeper in the nature of man, and to turn on some nobler hinge than the principle of hatred.

This person (who had thus, from the first moment of his entrance, struck in me what I

can only describe as a disgustful curiosity)
was dressed in a fashion that would have
made an ordinary person laughable ; his
clothes, that is to say, although they were of
rich and sober fabric, were enormously too
large for him in every measurement—the
trousers hanging on his legs and rolled up to
keep them from the ground, the waist of the
coat below his haunches, and the collar
sprawling wide upon his shoulders. Strange
to relate, this ludicrous accoutrement was far
from moving me to laughter. Rather, as
there was something abnormal and mis-
begotten in the very essence of the creature
that now faced me—something seizing, sur-
prising and revolting—this fresh disparity
seemed but to fit in with and to reinforce it ;
so that to my interest in the man's nature
and character, there was added a curiosity as
to his origin, his life, his fortune and status
in the world.

These observations, though they have
taken so great a space to be set down in,
were yet the work of a few seconds. My

visitor was, indeed, on fire with sombre excitement.

"Have you got it?" he cried. "Have you got it?" And so lively was his impatience that he even laid his hand upon my arm and sought to shake me.

I put him back, conscious at his touch of a certain icy pang along my blood. "Come, sir," said I. "You forget that I have not yet the pleasure of your acquaintance. Be seated, if you please." And I showed him an example, and sat down myself in my customary seat and with as fair an imitation of my ordinary manner to a patient, as the lateness of the hour, the nature of my pre-occupations, and the horror I had of my visitor, would suffer me to muster.

"I beg your pardon, Dr. Lanyon," he replied, civilly enough. "What you say is very well founded; and my impatience has shown its heels to my politeness. I come here at the instance of your colleague, Dr. Henry Jekyll, on a piece of business of some moment; and I understood . . ." he paused and put his hand to his throat, and I could see, in spite of his collected manner, that he was wrestling against the approaches of the hysteria—" I understood, a drawer . . ."

But here I took pity on my visitor's suspense, and some perhaps on my own growing curiosity.

" There it is, sir," said I, pointing to the drawer, where it lay on the floor behind a table, and still covered with the sheet.

He sprang to it, and then paused, and laid his hand upon his heart; I could hear his teeth grate with the convulsive action of his jaws; and his face was so ghastly to see that I grew alarmed both for his life and reason.

" Compose yourself," said I.

He turned a dreadful smile to me, and, as if with the decision of despair, plucked away the sheet. At sight of the contents, he uttered one loud sob of such immense relief that I sat petrified. And the next moment, in a voice that was already fairly well under control, " Have you a graduated glass?" he asked.

I rose from my place with something of an effort, and gave him what he asked.

He thanked me with a smiling nod, measured out a few minims of the red tinc‧ ture and added one of the powders. The mix‧ ture, which was at first of a reddish hue, be‧ gan, in proportion as the crystals melted, to brighten in colour, to effervesce audibly, and to throw off small fumes of vapour. Suddenly, and at the same moment, the ebullition ceased, and the compound changed to a dark purple, which faded again more slowly to a watery green. My visitor, who had watched these metamorphoses with a keen eye, smiled, set down the glass upon the table, and then turned and looked upon me with an air of scrutiny.

"And now," said he, "to settle what re‧ mains. Will you be wise? will you be guided? will you suffer me to take this glass in my hand, and to go forth from your house without further parley? or has the greed of curiosity too much command of you? Think before you answer, for it shall be done as you decide. As you decide, you shall be left as you were before, and neither richer nor wiser, unless the sense of service rendered to a man in mortal distress may be counted as a kind of riches of the soul. Or, if you shall so prefer to choose, a new province of knowledge and new avenues to fame and power shall be laid open to you, here, in this room, upon the instant; and your sight shall be blasted by a prodigy to stagger the unbelief of Satan."

"Sir," said I, affecting a coolness that I was far from truly possessing, "you speak enigmas, and you will perhaps not wonder that I hear you with no very strong impression of belief. But I have gone too far in the way of inexplicable services to pause before I see the end."

"It is well," replied my visitor. "Lanyon, you remember your vows: what follows is under the seal of our profession. And now, you who have so long been bound to the most narrow and material views, you who have denied the virtue of transcendental medicine, you who have derided your superiors—behold!"

He put the glass to his lips, and drank at one gulp. A cry followed; he reeled, staggered, clutched at the table and held on, staring with injected eyes, gasping with open mouth; and as I looked, there came, I thought, a change—he seemed to swell—his face became suddenly black, and the features seemed to melt and alter—and the next moment I had sprung to my feet and leaped back against the wall, my arm raised to shield me from that prodigy, my mind sub-merged in terror.

"O God!" I screamed, and "O God!" again and again; for there before my eyes— pale and shaken, and half fainting, and grop-ing before him with his hands, like a man restored from death—there stood Henry Jekyll!

What he told me in the next hour I can-not bring my mind to set on paper. I saw what I saw, I heard what I heard, and my soul sickened at it; and yet, now when that sight has faded from my eyes I ask myself if I believe it, and I cannot answer. My life is shaken to its roots; sleep has left me; the deadliest terror sits by me at all hours of the day and night; I feel that my days are numbered, and that I must die; and yet I shall die incredulous. As for the moral turpitude that man unveiled to me, even with tears of penitence, I cannot, even in memory, dwell on it without a start of horror. I will say but one thing, Utterson, and that (if you can bring your mind to credit it) will be more than enough. The creature who crept into my house that night was, on Jekyll's own confession, known by the name of Hyde and hunted for in every corner of the land as the murderer of Carew.

HASTIE LANYON.

HENRY JEKYLL'S FULL STATEMENT OF THE CASE.

I WAS born in the year 18— to a large fortune, endowed besides with excellent parts, inclined by nature to industry, fond of the respect of the wise and good among my fellow-men, and thus, as might have been supposed, with every guarantee of an honourable and distinguished future. And indeed, the worst of my faults was a certain impatient gaiety of disposition, such as has made the happiness of many, but such as I found it hard to reconcile with my imperious desire to carry my head high, and wear a more than commonly grave countenance before the public. Hence it came about that I concealed my pleasures; and that when I reached years of reflection, and began to look round me, and take stock of my progress and position in the world, I stood already committed to a profound duplicity of life. Many a man would have even blazoned such irregularities as I was guilty of; but from the high views that I had set before me, I regarded and hid them with an almost morbid sense of shame. It was thus rather the exacting nature of my aspirations, than any particular degradation in my faults, that made me what I was, and, with even a deeper trench than in the majority of men, severed in me those provinces of good and ill which divide and compound man's dual nature. In this case, I was driven to reflect deeply and inveterately on that hard law of life, which lies at the root of religion, and is one of the most plentiful springs of distress. Though so profound a double-dealer, I was in no sense a hypocrite; both sides of me were in dead earnest; I was no more myself when I laid aside restraint and plunged in shame, than when I laboured, in the eye of day, at the furtherance of knowledge or the relief of sorrow and suffering. And it chanced that the direction of my scientific studies, which led wholly towards the mystic and the transcendental, reacted and shed a strong light on this consciousness of the perennial war among my members. With every day, and from both sides of my intelligence, the moral and the intellectual, I thus drew steadily nearer to that truth, by whose partial discovery I have been doomed to such a dreadful shipwreck: that man is not truly one, but truly two. I say two, because the state of my own knowledge does not pass beyond that point. Others will follow, others will outstrip me on the same lines; and I hazard the guess that man will be ultimately known for a mere polity of multifarious, incongruous and independent denizens. I, for my part, from the nature of my life, advanced infallibly in one direction, and in one direction only. It was on the moral side, and in my own person, that I learned to recognise the thorough and primitive quality of man; I saw that, of the two natures that contended in the field of my consciousness, even if I could rightly be said to be either, it was only because I was radically both; and from an early date, even before the course of my scientific discoveries had begun to suggest the most naked possibility of such a miracle, I had learned to dwell with pleasure, as a beloved daydream, on the thought of the separation of these elements. If each, I told myself, could but be housed in separate identities, life would be relieved of all that was unbearable; the unjust might go his way, delivered from the aspirations and remorse of his more upright twin; and the just could walk steadfastly and securely on his upward path, doing the good things in which he found his pleasure, and no longer exposed to disgrace and penitence by the hands of this extraneous evil. It was the curse of mankind that these incongruous faggots were thus bound together—that in the agonised womb of consciousness, these polar twins should be continuously struggling. How, then, were they dissociated?

I was so far in my reflections, when, as I

have said, a side light began to shine upon
the subject from the laboratory table.   I began to perceive more deeply than it has ever
yet been stated, the trembling immateriality,
the mist-like transience, of this seemingly so
solid body in which we walk attired.   Certain agents I found to have the power to
shake and to pluck back that fleshly vest-
ment, even as a wind might toss the curtains
of a pavilion.   For two good reasons, I will
not enter deeply into this scientific branch of
my confession.   First, because I have been
made to learn that the doom and burthen of
our life is bound for ever on man's shoulders;
and when the attempt is made to cast it off,
it but returns upon us with more unfamiliar
and more awful pressure.   Second, because,
as my narrative will make, alas! too evident,
my discoveries were incomplete.   Enough,
then, that I not only recognised my natural
body from the mere aura and effulgence of
certain of the powers that made up my spirit,
but managed to compound a drug by which
these powers should be dethroned from their

supremacy, and a second form and countenance substituted, none the less natural to me because they were the expression, and bore the stamp, of lower elements in my soul.

I hesitated long before I put this theory to the test of practice. I knew well that I risked death; for any drug that so potently controlled and shook the very fortress of identity, might by the least scruple of an overdose or at the least inopportunity in the moment of exhibition, utterly blot out that immaterial tabernacle which I looked to it to change. But the temptation of a discovery so singular and profound, at last overcame the suggestions of alarm. I had long since prepared my tincture; I purchased at once, from a firm of wholesale chemists, a large quantity of a particular salt, which I knew, from my experiments, to be the last ingredient required; and, late one accursed night, I compounded the elements, watched them boil and smoke together in the glass, and when the ebullition had subsided, with a strong glow of courage, drank off the potion.

The most racking pangs succeeded: a grinding in the bones, deadly nausea, and a horror of the spirit that cannot be exceeded at the hour of birth or death. Then these agonies began swiftly to subside, and I came to myself as if out of a great sickness. There was something strange in my sensations, something indescribably new, and, from its very novelty, incredibly sweet. I felt younger, lighter, happier in body; within I was conscious of a heady recklessness, a current of disordered sensual images running like a mill race in my fancy, a solution of the bonds of obligation, an unknown but not an innocent freedom of the soul. I knew myself, at the first breath of this new life, to be more wicked, tenfold more wicked, sold a slave to my original evil; and the thought, in that moment, braced and delighted me like wine. I stretched out my hands, exulting in the freshness of these sensations; and in the act I was suddenly aware that I had lost in stature.

There was no mirror, at that date, in

my room ; that which stands beside me as I write was brought there later on, and for the very purpose of those transformations. The night, however, was far gone into the morning—the morning, black as it was, was nearly ripe for the conception of the day— the inmates of my house were locked in the most rigorous hours of slumber ; and I determined, flushed as I was with hope and triumph, to venture in my new shape as far as to my bedroom. I crossed the yard, wherein the constellations looked down upon me, I could have thought, with wonder, the first creature of that sort that their unsleeping vigilance had yet disclosed to them ; I stole through the corridors, a stranger in my own house ; and coming to my room, I saw for the first time the appearance of Edward Hyde.

I must here speak by theory alone, saying not that which I know, but that which I suppose to be most probable. The evil side of my nature, to which I had now transferred the stamping efficacy, was less robust and less developed than the good which I had just deposed. Again, in the course of my life, which had been, after all, nine-tenths a life of effort, virtue and control, it had been much less exercised and much less ex-hausted. And hence, as I think, it came about that Edward Hyde was so much smaller, slighter, and younger than Henry Jekyll. Even as good shone upon the countenance of the one, evil was written broadly and plainly on the face of the other. Evil besides (which I must still believe to be the lethal side of man) had left on that body an imprint of deformity and decay. And yet when I looked upon that ugly idol in the glass, I was conscious of no repugnance, rather of a leap of welcome. This, too, was myself. It seemed natural and human. In my eyes it bore a livelier image of the spirit, it seemed more express and single, than the imperfect and divided countenance I had been hitherto accustomed to call mine. And in so far I was doubtless right. I have observed that when I wore the semblance of Edward Hyde, none could come near to me at first without a visible misgiving of the flesh. This, as I take it, was because all human beings, as we meet them, are commingled out of good and evil: and Edward Hyde, alone, in the ranks of mankind, was pure evil.

I lingered but a moment at the mirror: the second and conclusive experiment had yet to be attempted; it yet remained to be seen if I had lost my identity beyond redemption and must flee before daylight from a house that was no longer mine: and hurrying back to my cabinet, I once more prepared and drank the cup, once more suffered the pangs of dissolution, and came to myself once more with the character, the stature, and the face of Henry Jekyll.

That night I had come to the fatal cross roads. Had I approached my discovery in a more noble spirit, had I risked the experiment while under the empire of generous or pious aspirations, all must have been otherwise, and from these agonies of death and

' birth I had come forth an angel instead of a fiend. The drug had no discriminating action; it was neither diabolical nor divine; it but shook the doors of the prison-house of my disposition; and, like the captives of Philippi, that which stood within ran forth. At that time my virtue slumbered; my evil, kept awake by ambition, was alert and swift to seize the occasion; and the thing that was projected was Edward Hyde. Hence, although I had now two characters as well as two appearances, one was wholly evil, and the other was still the old Henry Jekyll, that incongruous compound of whose reformation and improvement I had already learned to despair. The movement was thus wholly toward the worse.

Even at that time, I had not yet conquered my aversion to the dryness of a life of study. I would still be merrily disposed at times; and as my pleasures were (to say the least) undignified, and I was not only well known and highly considered, but growing towards the elderly man, this incoherency of my life was daily growing more unwelcome. It was on this side that my new power tempted me until I fell in slavery. I had but to drink the cup, to doff at once the body of the noted professor, and to assume, like a thick cloak, that of Edward Hyde. I smiled at the notion; it seemed to me at the time to be humorous; and I made my preparations with the most studious care. I took and furnished that house in Soho, to which Hyde was tracked by the police; and engaged as housekeeper a creature whom I well knew to be silent and unscrupulous. On the other side, I announced to my servants that a Mr. Hyde (whom I described) was to have full liberty and power about my house in the square; and, to parry mishaps, I even called and made myself a familiar object, in my second character. I next drew up that will to which you so much objected; so that if anything befell me in the person of Dr. Jekyll, I could enter on that of Edward Hyde without pecuniary loss. And thus fortified, as I supposed, on every side,

I began to profit by the strange immunities of my position.

Men have before hired bravos to transact their crimes, while their own person and reputation sat under shelter. I was the first that ever did so for his pleasures. I was the first that could thus plod in the public eye with a load of genial respectability, and in a moment, like a schoolboy, strip off these lendings and spring headlong into the sea of liberty. But for me, in my impenetrable mantle, the safety was complete. Think of it—I did not even exist! Let me but escape into my laboratory door, give me but a second or two to mix and swallow the draught that I had always standing ready; and, whatever he had done, Edward Hyde would pass away like the stain of breath upon a mirror; and there in his stead, quietly at home, trimming the midnight lamp in his study, a man who could afford to laugh at suspicion, would be Henry Jekyll.

The pleasures which I made haste to seek

in my disguise were, as I have said, undignified; I would scarce use a harder term.
But in the hands of Edward Hyde, they
soon began to turn towards the monstrous.
When I would come back from these excursions, I was often plunged into a kind of
wonder at my vicarious depravity. This
familiar that I called out of my own soul,
and sent forth alone to do his good pleasure,
was a being inherently malign and villainous;
his every act and thought centred on self;
drinking pleasure with bestial avidity from
any degree of torture to another; relentless
like a man of stone. Henry Jekyll stood
at times aghast before the acts of Edward
Hyde; but the situation was apart from ordinary laws, and insidiously relaxed the
grasp of conscience. It was Hyde, after
all, and Hyde alone, that was guilty. Jekyll
was no worse; he woke again to his good
qualities seemingly unimpaired; he would
even make haste, where it was possible, to
undo the evil done by Hyde. And thus
his conscience slumbered.

Into the details of the infamy at which I thus connived (for even now I can scarce grant that I committed it) I have no design of entering ; I mean but to point out the warnings and the successive steps with which my chastisement approached. I met with one accident which, as it brought on no consequence, I shall no more than mention. An act of cruelty to a child aroused against me the anger of a passer-by, whom I recognised the other day in the person of your kinsman ; the doctor and the child's family joined him ; there were moments when I feared for my life ; and at last, in order to pacify their too just resentment, Edward Hyde had to bring them to the door, and pay them in a cheque drawn in the name of Henry Jekyll. But this danger was easily eliminated from the future, by opening an account at another bank in the name of Edward Hyde himself ; and when, by sloping my own hand backwards, I had supplied my double with a signature, I thought I sat beyond the reach of fate.

Some two months before the murder of Sir Danvers, I had been out for one of my adventures, had returned at a late hour, and woke the next day in bed with somewhat odd sensations. It was in vain I looked about me; in vain I saw the decent furniture and tall proportions of my room in the square; in vain that I recognised the pattern of the bed curtains and the design of the mahogany frame; something still kept insisting that I was not where I was, that I had not wakened where I seemed to be, but in the little room in Soho where I was accustomed to sleep in the body of Edward Hyde. I smiled to myself, and, in my psychological way, began lazily to inquire into the elements of this illusion, occasionally, even as I did so, dropping back into a comfortable morning doze. I was still so engaged when, in one of my more wakeful moments, my eye fell upon my hand. Now, the hand of Henry Jekyll (as you have often remarked) was professional in shape and size; it was large, firm, white and comely. But

the hand which I now saw, clearly enough,
in the yellow light of a mid-London morning,
lying half shut on the bedclothes, was lean,
corded, knuckly, of a dusky pallor, and thickly
shaded with a swart growth of hair.   It
was the hand of Edward Hyde.

I must have stared upon it for near half
a minute, sunk as I was in the mere stupidity
of wonder, before terror woke up in my
breast as sudden and startling as the crash
of cymbals; and bounding from my bed,
I rushed to the mirror.   At the sight that
met my eyes, my blood was changed into
something exquisitely thin and icy.   Yes, I
had gone to bed Henry Jekyll, I had
awakened Edward Hyde How was this
to be explained? I asked myself; and then,
with another bound of terror—how was it
to be remedied?   It was well on in the
morning; the servants were up; all my
drugs were in the cabinet—a long journey,
down two pair of stairs, through the back
passage, across the open court and through
the anatomical theatre, from where I was

then standing horror-struck. It might indeed be possible to cover my face; but of what use was that, when I was unable to conceal the alteration in my stature? And then, with an overpowering sweetness of relief, it came back upon my mind that the servants were already used to the coming and going of my second self. I had soon dressed, as well as I was able, in clothes of my own size: had soon passed through the house, where Bradshaw stared and drew back at seeing Mr. Hyde at such an hour and in such a strange array; and ten minutes later, Dr. Jekyll had returned to his own shape, and was sitting down, with a darkened brow, to make a feint of breakfasting.

Small indeed was my appetite. This inexplicable incident, this reversal of my previous experience, seemed, like the Babylonian finger on the wall, to be spelling out the letters of my judgment; and I began to reflect more seriously than ever before on the issues and possibilities of my double existence. That part of me which I had the

power of projecting had lately been much
exercised and nourished; it had seemed to
me of late as though the body of Edward
Hyde had grown in stature, as though (when
I wore that form) I were conscious of a
more generous tide of blood; and I began
to spy a danger that, if this were much pro-
longed, the balance of my nature might be
permanently overthrown, the power of
voluntary change be forfeited, and the
character of Edward Hyde become irrevoc-
ably mine. The power of the drug had not
been always equally displayed. Once, very
early in my career, it had totally failed me;
since then I had been obliged on more than
one occasion to double, and once, with
infinite risk of death, to treble the amount;
and these rare uncertainties had cast hitherto
the sole shadow on my contentment. Now,
however, and in the light of that morning's
accident, I was led to remark that whereas,
in the beginning, the difficulty had been to
throw off the body of Jekyll, it had of late
gradually but decidedly transferred itself to

the other side. All things therefore seemed to point to this: that I was slowly losing hold of my original and better self, and becoming slowly incorporated with my second and worse.

Between these two, I now felt I had to choose. My two natures had memory in common, but all other faculties were most unequally shared between them. Jekyll (who was composite) now with the most sensitive apprehensions, now with a greedy gusto, projected and shared in the pleasures and adventures of Hyde; but Hyde was indifferent to Jekyll, or but remembered him as the mountain bandit remembers the cavern in which he conceals himself from pursuit. Jekyll had more than a father's interest; Hyde had more than a son's indifference. To cast in my lot with Jekyll was to die to those appetites which I had long secretly indulged and had of late begun to pamper. To cast it in with Hyde was to die to a thousand interests and aspirations, and to become, at a blow and for ever,

despised and friendless.   The bargain might
appear unequal ; but there was still another
consideration in the scales ; for while Jekyll
would suffer smartingly in the fires of
abstinence, Hyde would be not even conscious of all that he had lost.   Strange as
my circumstances were, the terms of this
debate are as old and commonplace as
man ; much the same inducements and
alarms cast the die for any tempted and
trembling sinner ; and it fell out with me,
as it falls with so vast a majority of my
fellows, that I chose the better part, and
was found wanting in the strength to keep
to it.

Yes, I preferred the elderly and discon-
tented doctor, surrounded by friends, and
cherishing honest hopes ; and bade a resolute
farewell to the liberty, the comparative
youth, the light step, leaping pulses and
secret pleasures, that I had enjoyed in the
disguise of Hyde.   I made this choice perhaps with some unconscious reservation, for
I neither gave up the house in Soho, nor de-

stroyed the clothes of Edward Hyde, which still lay ready in my cabinet   For two months, however, I was true to my determination; for two months I led a life of such severity as I had never before attained to, and enjoyed the compensations of an approving conscience.   But time began at last to obliterate the freshness of my alarm; the praises of conscience began to grow into a thing of course; I began to be tortured with throes and longings, as of Hyde struggling after freedom; and at last, in an hour of moral weakness, I once again compounded and swallowed the transforming draught.

I do not suppose that when a drunkard reasons with himself upon his vice, he is once out of five hundred times affected by the dangers that he runs through his brutish physical insensibility; neither had I, long as I had considered my position, made enough allowance for the complete moral insensibility and insensate readiness to evil, which were the leading characters of Edward Hyde. Yet it was by these that I was punished.

My devil had been long caged, he came out roaring. I was conscious, even when I took the draught, of a more unbridled, a more furious propensity to ill. It must have been this, I suppose, that stirred in my soul that tempest of impatience with which I listened to the civilities of my unhappy victim; I declare at least, before God, no man morally sane could have been guilty of that crime upon so pitiful a provocation; and that I struck in no more reasonable spirit than that in which a sick child may break a plaything. But I had voluntarily stripped myself of all those balancing instincts by which even the worst of us continues to walk with some degree of steadiness among temptations; and in my case, to be tempted, however slightly, was to fall.

Instantly the spirit of hell awoke in me and raged. With a transport of glee, I mauled the unresisting body, tasting delight from every blow; and it was not till weariness had begun to succeed that I was suddenly, in the top fit of my delirium, struck through the heart by a cold thrill of terror. A mist dispersed; I saw my life to be forfeit; and fled from the scene of these excesses, at once glorying and trembling, my lust of evil gratified and stimulated, my love of life screwed to the topmost peg. I ran to the house in Soho, and (to make assurance doubly sure) destroyed my papers; thence I set out through the lamplit streets, in the same divided ecstasy of mind, gloating on my crime, light-headedly devising others in the future, and yet still hastening and still hearkening in my wake for the steps of the avenger. Hyde had a song upon his lips as he compounded the draught, and as he drank it pledged the dead man. The pangs of transformation had not done tearing him, before Henry Jekyll, with streaming tears of gratitude and remorse, had fallen upon his knees and lifted his clasped hands to God. The veil of self-indulgence was rent from head to foot, I saw my life as a whole: I followed it up from the days of childhood, when I had walked with my father's hand, and

through the self-denying toils of. my professional life, to arrive again and again, with
the same sense of unreality, at the damned
horrors of the evening. I could have
screamed aloud; I sought with tears and
prayers to smother down the crowd of
hideous images and sounds with which my
memory swarmed against me ; and still, between the petitions, the ugly face of my iniquity stared into my soul. As the acuteness
of this remorse began to die away, it was
succeeded by a sense of joy. The problem
of my conduct was solved. Hyde was
thenceforth impossible ; whether I would or
not, I was now confined to the better part of
my existence; and, oh, how I rejoiced to
think it! with what willing humility I em-
braced anew the restrictions of natural life!
with what sincere renunciation I locked the
door by which I had so often gone and
come, and ground the key under my heel!

The next day came the news that the
murder had been overlooked, that the guilt
of Hyde was patent to the world, and that

the victim was a man high in public estima-
tion. It was not only a crime, it had been a
tragic folly. I think I was glad to know it;
I think I was glad to have my better im-
pulses thus buttressed and guarded by the
terrors of the scaffold. Jekyll was now my
city of refuge; let but Hyde peep out an
instant, and the hands of all men would be
raised to take and slay him.

I resolved in my future conduct to redeem
the past; and I can say with honesty that
my resolve was fruitful of some good. You
know yourself how earnestly in the last
months of last year I laboured to relieve
suffering; you know that much was done for
others, and that the days passed quietly, almost happily for myself. Nor can I truly
say that I wearied of this beneficent and
innocent life; I think instead that I daily
enjoyed it more completely; but I was still
cursed with my duality of purpose; and as
the first edge of my penitence wore off, the
lower side of me, so long indulged, so recently chained down, began to growl for

license. Not that I dreamed of resuscitat-
ing Hyde; the bare idea of that would
startle me to frenzy: no, it was in my own
person that I was once more tempted to
trifle with my conscience; and it was as an
ordinary secret sinner that I at last fell before the assaults of temptation.

There comes an end to all things; the
most capacious measure is filled at last; and
this brief condescension to my evil finally
destroyed the balance of my soul. And yet
I was not alarmed; the fall seemed natural,
like a return to the old days before I had
made my discovery. It was a fine, clear
January day, wet under foot where the
frost had melted, but cloudless overhead;
and the Regent's Park was full of winter
chirrupings and sweet with spring odours.
I sat in the sun on a bench; the animal
within me licking the chops of memory; the
spiritual side a little drowsed, promising
subsequent penitence, but not yet moved to
begin. After all, I reflected I was like my
neighbours; and then I smiled, comparing

myself with other men, comparing my active goodwill with the lazy cruelty of their neglect. And at the very moment of that vainglorious thought, a qualm came over me, a horrid nausea and the most deadly shuddering. These passed away, and left me faint; and then as in its turn the faintness subsided, I began to be aware of a change in the temper of my thoughts, a greater boldness, a contempt of danger, a solution of the bonds of obligation. I looked down; my clothes hung formlessly on my shrunken limbs; the hand that lay on my knee was corded and hairy. I was once more Edward Hyde. A moment before I had been safe of all men's respect, wealthy, beloved—the cloth laying for me in the dining-room at home; and now I was the common quarry of mankind, hunted, houseless, a known murderer, thrall to the gallows.

My reason wavered, but it did not fail me utterly. I have more than once observed that, in my second character, my faculties

seemed sharpened to a point and my spirits
more tensely elastic ; thus it came about
that, where Jekyll perhaps might have suc-
cumbed, Hyde rose to the importance of
the moment.   My drugs were in one of the
presses of my cabinet : how was I to reach
them ?   That was the problem that (crushing my temples in my hands) I set myself to
solve.   The laboratory door I had closed.
If I sought to enter by the house, my own
servants would consign me to the gallows.
I saw I must employ another hand, and
thought of Lanyon.   How was he to be
reached ? how persuaded ?   Supposing that
I escaped capture in the streets, how was I
to make my way into his presence ? and
how should I, an unknown and displeasing
visitor, prevail on the famous physician to
rifle the study of his colleague, Dr. Jekyll ?
Then I remembered that of my original character, one part remained to me : I could write
my own hand ; and once I had conceived
that kindling spark, the way that I must
follow became lighted up from end to end.

Thereupon, I arranged my clothes as best I could, and summoning a passing hansom, drove to an hotel in Portland Street, the name of which I chanced to remember. At my appearance (which was indeed comical enough, however tragic a fate these garments covered) the driver could not conceal his mirth. I gnashed my teeth upon him with a gust of devilish fury; and the smile withered from his face—happily for him— yet more happily for myself, for in another instant I had certainly dragged him from his perch. At the inn, as I entered, I looked about me with so black a countenance as made the attendants tremble; not a look did they exchange in my presence; but obsequiously took my orders, led me to a private room, and brought me wherewithal to write. Hyde in danger of his life was a creature new to me: shaken with inordinate anger, strung to the pitch of murder, lusting to inflict pain. Yet the creature was astute; mastered his fury with a great effort of the will; composed his two important letters, one to Lanyon and one to Poole; and, that he might receive actual evidence of their being posted, sent them out with directions that they should be registered.

Thenceforward, he sat all day over the fire in the private room, gnawing his nails; there he dined, sitting alone with his fears, the waiter visibly quailing before his eye; and thence, when the night was fully come, he set forth in the corner of a closed cab, and was driven to and fro about the streets of the city. He, I say—I cannot say, I. That child of Hell had nothing human; nothing lived in him but fear and hatred. And when at last, thinking the driver had begun to grow suspicious, he discharged the cab and ventured on foot, attired in his misfitting clothes, an object marked out for observation, into the midst of the nocturnal passengers, these two base passions raged within him like a tempest. He walked fast, hunted by his fears, chattering to himself, skulking through the less frequented thoroughfares, counting the minutes that still divided him from midnight. Once a woman spoke to him, offering, I think, a box of lights. He smote her in the face, and she fled.

When I came to myself at Lanyon's, the horror of my old friend perhaps affected me somewhat: I do not know; it was at least but a drop in the sea to the abhorrence with which I looked back upon these hours. A change had come over me. It was no longer the fear of the gallows, it was the horror of being Hyde that racked me. I received Lanyon's condemnation partly in a dream; it was partly in a dream that I came home to my own house and got into bed. I slept after the prostration of the day, with a stringent and profound slumber which not even the nightmares that wrung me could avail to break. I awoke in the morning shaken, weakened, but refreshed. I still hated and feared the thought of the brute that slept within me, and I had not of course forgotten the appal·

ling dangers of the day before; but I was
once more at home, in my own house and
close to my drugs; and gratitude for my
escape shone so strong in my soul that it
almost rivalled the brightness of hope.

I was stepping leisurely across the court
after breakfast, drinking the chill of the air
with pleasure, when I was seized again with
those indescribable sensations that heralded
the change; and I had but the time to gain
the shelter of my cabinet, before I was once
again raging and freezing with the passions
of Hyde. It took on this occasion a double
dose to recall me to myself; and, alas! six
hours after, as I sat looking sadly in the
fire, the pangs returned, and the drug had
to be re-administered. In short, from that
day forth it seemed only by a great effort
as of gymnastics, and only under the im-
mediate stimulation of the drug, that I was
able to wear the countenance of Jekyll.
At all hours of the day and night I would
be taken with the premonitory shudder;
above all, if I slept, or even dozed for a

moment in my chair, it was always as
Hyde that I awakened. Under the strain
of this continually impending doom and by
the sleeplessness to which I now condemned
myself, ay, even beyond what I had thought
possible to man, I became, in my own person,
a creature eaten up and emptied by fever,
languidly weak both in body and mind, and
solely occupied by one thought: the horror
of my other self. But when I slept, or
when the virtue of the medicine wore off,
I would leap almost without transition (for
the pangs of transformation grew daily less
marked) into the possession of a fancy
brimming with images of terror, a soul
boiling with causeless hatreds, and a body
that seemed not strong enough to contain
the raging energies of life. The powers of
Hyde seemed to have grown with the sick-
liness of Jekyll. And certainly the hate
that now divided them was equal on each
side. With Jekyll, it was a thing of vital
instinct. He had now seen the full deformity
of that creature that shared with him some

of the phenomena of consciousness, and was co-heir with him to death : and beyond these links of community, which in themselves made the most poignant part of his distress, he thought of Hyde, for all his energy of life, as of something not only hellish but inorganic. This was the shocking thing ; that the slime of the pit seemed to utter cries and voices ; that the amorphous dust gesticulated and sinned ; that what was dead, and had no shape, should usurp the offices of life. And this again, that that insurgent horror was knit to him closer than a wife, closer than an eye ; lay caged in his flesh, where he heard it mutter and felt it struggle to be born ; and at every hour of weakness, and in the confidence of slumber, prevailed against him, and deposed him out of life. The hatred of Hyde for Jekyll was of a different order. His terror of the gallows drove him continually to commit temporary suicide, and return to his subordinate station of a part instead of a person ; but he loathed the necessity, he loathed the despondency into which Jekyll was now fallen, and he resented the dislike with which he was himself regarded. Hence the apelike tricks that he would play me, scrawling in my own hand blasphemies on the pages of my books, burning the letters and destroying the portrait of my father; and indeed, had it not been for his fear of death, he would long ago have ruined himself in order to involve me in the ruin. But his love of life is wonderful; I go further: I, who sicken and freeze at the mere thought of him, when I recall the abjection and passion of this attachment, and when I know how he fears my power to cut him off by suicide, I find it in my heart to pity him.

It is useless, and the time awfully fails me, to prolong this description; no one has ever suffered such torments, let that suffice; and yet even to these, habit brought—no, not alleviation—but a certain callousness of soul, a certain acquiescence of despair; and

my punishment might have gone on for
years, but for the last calamity which has
now fallen, and which has finally severed
me from my own face and nature. My
provision of the salt, which had never been
renewed since the date of the first experiment, began to run low. I sent out for a
fresh supply, and mixed the draught; the
ebullition followed, and the first change of
colour, not the second; I drank it, and it
was without efficiency. You will learn
from Poole how I have had London ransacked; it was in vain; and I am now persuaded that my first supply was impure, and
that it was that unknown impurity which
lent efficacy to the draught.

About a week has passed, and I am now
finishing this statement under the influence of
the last of the old powders. This, then, is
the last time, short of a miracle, that Henry
Jekyll can think his own thoughts or see his
own face (now how sadly altered!) in the
glass. Nor must I delay too long to bring
my writing to an end; for if my narrative

has hitherto escaped destruction, it has been by a combination of great prudence and great good luck. Should the throes of change take me in the act of writing it, Hyde will tear it in pieces; but if some time shall have elapsed after I have laid it by, his wonderful selfishness and circumscription to the moment will probably save it once again from the action of his apelike spite. And indeed the doom that is closing on us both has already changed and crushed him. Half an hour from now, when I shall again and for ever reindue that hated personality, I know how I shall sit shuddering and weeping in my chair, or continue, with the most strained and fearstruck ecstasy of listening, to pace up and down this room (my last earthly refuge) and give ear to every sound of menace. Will Hyde die upon the scaffold? or will he find the courage to release himself at the last moment? God knows; I am careless; this is my true hour of death, and what is to follow concerns another than myself.

Here, then, as I lay down the pen, and proceed to seal up my confession, I bring the life of that unhappy Henry Jekyll to an end.

FABLES.[*]

THE fable, as a form of literary art, had at all times a great attraction for Mr. Stevenson; and in an early review of Lord Lytton's *Fables in Song* he attempted to define some of its proper aims and methods. To this class of work, according to his conception of the matter, belonged essentially several of his own semi-supernatural stories, such as "Will of the Mill," "Markheim," and even "Jekyll and Hyde"; in the composition of which there was combined with the dream element, in at least an equal measure, the element of moral allegory or apologue. He was accustomed also to try his hand occasionally on the composition of fables more strictly so called, and cast in the conventional brief and familiar form. By the winter of 1887-88 he had enough of these by him, together with a few others running to greater length, and conceived in a more mystic and legendary vein, to enable him, as he thought, to see his way towards making a book of them. Such a book he promised to Messrs. Longman on the occasion of a visit paid him in New York

* Copyright 1896, by Longmans, Green, and Co.

by a member of the firm in the spring of 1888. Then
came his voyage in the Pacific and residence at Samoa.
Among the multitude of new interests and images
which filled his mind during the last six years of his
life, he seems to have given little thought to the pro-
posed book of fables. One or two, however, as will
be seen, were added to the collection during this period.
That collection, as it stood at the time of his death,
was certainly not what its author had meant it to be.
It may even be doubted whether it would have seen
the light had he lived: but since his death it has
seemed to his representatives of sufficient interest
to be handed to Messrs. Longman, in part fulfilment
of his old pledge to them, for publication first in
their Magazine, and afterwards in its present place
as an appendix to a new edition of "The Strange Case
of Dr. Jekyll and Mr. Hyde".

S. C.

I.

THE PERSONS OF THE TALE.

AFTER the 32nd chapter of *Treasure Island*, two of the puppets strolled out to have a pipe before business should begin again, and met in an open place not far from the story.

"Good-morning, Cap'n," said the first, with a man-o'-war salute, and a beaming countenance.

"Ah, Silver!" grunted the other. "You're in a bad way, Silver."

"Now, Cap'n Smollett," remonstrated Silver, "dooty is dooty, as I knows, and none better; but we're off dooty now; and I can't see no call to keep up the morality business."

"You're a damned rogue, my man," said the Captain.

"Come, come, Cap'n, be just," returned the other. "There's no call to be angry with me in earnest. I'm on'y a chara'ter in a sea story. I don't really exist."

"Well, I don't really exist either," says the Captain, "which seems to meet that."

"I wouldn't set no limits to what a virtuous chara'ter might consider argument," responded Silver. "But I'm the villain of this tale, I am; and speaking as one seafaring man to another, what I want to know is, what's the odds?"

"Were you never taught your catechism?" said the Captain. "Don't you know there's such a thing as an Author?"

"Such a thing as a Author?" returned John, derisively. "And who better'n me? And the p'int is, if the Author made you, he made Long John, and he made Hands, and Pew, and George Merry—not that George is up to much, for he's little more'n a name; and he made Flint, what there is of him; and he made this here mutiny, you keep such a work about; and he had Tom Redruth shot; and—well, if that's a Author, give me Pew!"

"Don't you believe in a future state?" said Smollett. "Do you think there's nothing but the present story-paper?"

"I don't rightly know for that," said Silver; "and I don't see what it's got to do with it, anyway. What I know is this: if there is sich a thing as a Author, I'm his favourite chara'ter. He does me fathoms better'n he does you—fathoms, he does. And he likes doing me. He keeps me on deck mostly all the time, crutch and all; and he leaves you measling in the hold, where nobody can't see you, nor wants to, and you may lay to that! If there is a Author, by thunder, but he's on my side, and you may lay to it!"

"I see he's giving you a long rope," said the Captain. "But that can't change a man's convictions. I know the Author respects me; I feel it in my bones; when you and I had that talk at the blockhouse door, who do you think he was for, my man?"

" And don't he respect me ? " cried Silver. " Ah, you should 'a' heard me putting down my mutiny, George Merry and Morgan and that lot, no longer ago'n last chapter ; you'd 'a' heard something then ! You'd 'a' seen what the Author thinks o' me ! But come now, do you consider yourself a virtuous chara'ter clean through ? "

" God forbid ! " said Captain Smollett, solemnly. " I am a man that tries to do his duty, and makes a mess of it as often as not. I'm not a very popular man at home, Silver, I'm afraid ! " and the Captain sighed.

" Ah," says Silver. " Then how about this sequel of yours ? Are you to be Cap'n Smollett just the same as ever, and not very popular at home, says you ? And if so, why, it's *Treasure Island* over again, by thunder ; and I'll be Long John, and Pew'll be Pew, and we'll have another mutiny, as like as not. Or are you to be somebody else ? And if so, why, what the better are you ? and what the worse am I ? "

" Why, look here, my man," returned the

Captain, "I can't understand how this story comes about at all, can I? I can't see how you and I, who don't exist, should get to speaking here, and smoke our pipes for all the world like reality? Very well, then, who am I to pipe up with my opinions? I know the Author's on the side of good; he tells me so, it runs out of his pen as he writes. Well, that's all I need to know; I'll take my chance upon the rest."

"It's a fact he seemed to be against George Merry," Silver admitted, musingly. "But George is little more'n a name at the best of it," he added, brightening. "And to get into soundings for once. What is this good? I made a mutiny, and I been a gentleman o' fortune; well, but by all stories, you ain't no such saint. I'm a man that keeps company very easy; even by your own account, you ain't, and to my certain knowledge you're a devil to haze. Which is which? Which is good, and which bad? Ah, you tell me that! Here we are in stays, and you may lay to it!"

"We're none of us perfect," replied the Captain. "That's a fact of religion, my man. All I can say is, I try to do my duty; and if you try to do yours, I can't compliment you on your success."

"And so you was the judge, was you?" said Silver, derisively.

"I would be both judge and hangman for you, my man, and never turn a hair," returned the Captain. "But I get beyond that: it mayn't be sound theology, but it's common sense, that what is good is useful too—or there and thereabout, for I don't set up to be a thinker. Now, where would a story go to if there were no virtuous characters?"

"If you go to that," replied Silver, "where would a story begin, if there wasn't no villains?"

"Well, that's pretty much my thought," said Captain Smollett. "The Author has to get a story; that's what he wants; and to get a story, and to have a man like the doctor (say) given a proper chance, he has to put in men like you and Hands. But he's on the right side; and you mind your eye! You're not through this story yet; there's trouble coming for you."

" What'll you bet?" asked John.

" Much I care if there ain't," returned the Captain. " I'm glad enough to be Alexander Smollett, bad as he is; and I thank my stars upon my knees that I'm not Silver. But there's the ink-bottle opening. To quarters!"

And indeed the Author was just then beginning to write the words:

CHAPTER XXXIII.

II.

THE SINKING SHIP.

"Sir," said the first lieutenant, bursting into the Captain's cabin, "the ship is going down."

"Very well, Mr. Spoker," said the Captain; "but that is no reason for going about half-shaved. Exercise your mind a moment, Mr. Spoker, and you will see that to the philosophic eye there is nothing new in our position: the ship (if she is to go down at all) may be said to have been going down since she was launched."

"She is settling fast," said the first lieutenant, as he returned from shaving.

"Fast, Mr. Spoker?" asked the Captain. "The expression is a strange one, for time (if you will think of it) is only relative."

"Sir," said the lieutenant, "I think it is

scarcely worth while to embark in such a discussion when we shall all be in Davy Jones's Locker in ten minutes."

" By parity of reasoning," returned the Captain gently, " it would never be worth while to begin any inquiry of importance ; the odds are always overwhelming that we must die before we shall have brought it to an end. You have not considered, Mr. Spoker, the situation of man," said the Captain, smiling, and shaking his head.

" I am much more engaged in considering the position of the ship," said Mr. Spoker.

" Spoken like a good officer," replied the Captain, laying his hand on the lieutenant's shoulder.

On deck they found the men had broken into the spirit-room, and were fast getting drunk.

"My men," said the Captain, "there is no sense in this. The ship is going down, you will tell me, in ten minutes : well, and what then ? To the philosophic eye, there is nothing new in our position. All our lives long, we may have been about to break a blood-vessel or to be struck by lightning, not merely in ten minutes, but in ten seconds ; and that has not prevented us from eating dinner, no, nor from putting money in the Savings Bank. I assure you, with my hand on my heart, I fail to comprehend your attitude."

The men were already too far gone to pay much heed.

" This is a very painful sight, M Spoker," said the Captain.

" And yet to the philosophic eye, or whatever it is," replied the first lieutenant, " they may be said to have been getting drunk since they came aboard."

" I do not know if you always follow my thought, Mr. Spoker," returned the Captain gently. " But let us proceed."

In the powder magazine they found an old salt smoking his pipe.

" Good God," cried the Captain, " what are you about ? "

" Well, sir," said the old salt, apologetically, "they told me as she were going down."

" And suppose she were ? " said the Captain. " To the philosophic eye, there would be nothing new in our position. Life, my old shipmate, life, at any moment and in any view, is as dangerous as a sinking ship ; and yet it is man's handsome fashion to carry umbrellas, to wear indiarubber over-shoes, to begin vast works, and to conduct himself in every way as if he might hope to be eternal. And for my own poor part I should despise the man who, even on board a sinking ship, should omit to take a pill or to wind up his watch. That, my friend, would not be the human attitude."

" I beg pardon, sir," said Mr. Spoker. " But what is precisely the difference be-tween shaving in a sinking ship and smok-ing in a powder magazine ? "

" Or doing anything at all in any con-ceivable circumstances ? " cried the Captain. " Perfectly conclusive ; give me a cigar ! "

Two minutes afterwards the ship blew up with a glorious detonation.

ONE day there was a traveller in the woods in California, in the dry season, when the Trades were blowing strong. He had ridden a long way, and he was tired and hungry, and dismounted from his horse to smoke a pipe. But when he felt in his pocket he found but two matches. He struck the first, and it would not light.

"Here is a pretty state of things!" said the traveller. "Dying for a smoke; only one match left; and that certain to miss fire! Was there ever a creature so unfortunate? And yet," thought the traveller, "suppose I light this match, and smoke my pipe, and shake out the dottle here in the grass—the grass might catch on fire, for it is dry like tinder; and while I snatch out the flames in front, they might evade and run behind me, and seize upon yon bush of poison oak ; before I could reach it, that would have blazed up ; over the bush I see a pine tree hung with moss ; that too would fly in fire upon the instant to its topmost bough ; and the flame of that long torch—how would the trade wind take and brandish that through the inflammable forest ! I hear this dell roar in a moment with the joint voice of wind and fire, I see myself gallop for my soul, and the flying conflagration chase and outflank me through the hills; I see this pleasant forest burn for days, and the cattle roasted, and the springs dried up, and the farmer ruined, and his children cast upon the world. What a world hangs upon this moment !"

With that he struck the match, and it missed fire.

" Thank God !" said the traveller, and put his pipe in his pocket.

IV.

THE SICK MAN AND THE FIREMAN.

THERE was once a sick man in a burning house, to whom there entered a fireman.

"Do not save me," said the sick man. "Save those who are strong."

"Will you kindly tell me why?" inquired the fireman, for he was a civil fellow.

"Nothing could possibly be fairer," said the sick man. "The strong should be preferred in all cases, because they are of more service in the world."

The fireman pondered a while, for he was a man of some philosophy. "Granted," said he at last, as a part of the roof fell in; "but for the sake of conversation, what would you lay down as the proper service of the strong?"

"Nothing can possibly be easier," returned

the sick man; "the proper service of the strong is to help the weak."

Again the fireman reflected, for there was nothing hasty about this excellent creature. "I could forgive you being sick," he said at last, as a portion of the wall fell out, "but I cannot bear your being such a fool." And with that he heaved up his fireman's axe, for he was eminently just, and clove the sick man to the bed.

V.

THE DEVIL AND THE INNKEEPER.

ONCE upon a time the devil stayed at an inn, where no one knew him, for they were people whose education had been neglected. He was bent on mischief, and for a time kept everybody by the ears. But at last the innkeeper set a watch upon the devil and took him in the fact.

The innkeeper got a rope's end.

"Now I am going to thrash you," said the innkeeper.

"You have no right to be angry with me," said the devil. "I am only the devil, and it is my nature to do wrong."

"Is that so?" asked the innkeeper.

"Fact, I assure you," said the devil.

"You really cannot help doing ill?" asked the innkeeper.

" Not in the smallest," said the devil ; " it would be useless cruelty to thrash a thing like me."

" It would indeed," said the innkeeper.

And he made a noose and hanged the devil.

" There!" said the innkeeper.

VI.

THE PENITENT.

A MAN met a lad weeping. "What do you weep for?" he asked.

"I am weeping for my sins," said the lad.

"You must have little to do," said the man.

The next day they met again. Once more the lad was weeping. "Why do you weep now?" asked the man.

"I am weeping because I have nothing to eat," said the lad.

"I thought it would come to that," said the man.

VII.

THE YELLOW PAINT.

In a certain city there lived a physician who sold yellow paint. This was of so singular a virtue that whoso was bedaubed with it from head to heel was set free from the dangers of life, and the bondage of sin, and the fear of death for ever. So the physician said in his prospectus; and so said all the citizens in the city; and there was nothing more urgent in men's hearts than to be properly painted themselves, and nothing they took more delight in than to see others painted. There was in the same city a young man of a very good family but of a somewhat reckless life, who had reached the age of manhood, and would have nothing to say to the paint: "To-morrow was soon enough," said he; and when the morrow came he would still put it off. She might have continued to do until his death; only, he had a friend of about his own age and much of his own manners; and this youth, taking a walk in the public street, with not one fleck of paint upon his body, was suddenly run down by a water-cart and cut off in the heyday of his nakedness. This shook the other to the soul; so that I never beheld a man more earnest to be painted; and on the very same evening, in the presence of all his family, to appropriate music, and himself weeping aloud, he received three complete coats and a touch of varnish on the top. The physician (who was himself affected even to tears) protested he had never done a job so thorough.

Some two months afterwards, the young man was carried on a stretcher to the physician's house.

"What is the meaning of this?" he cried, as soon as the door was opened. "I was to be set free from all the dangers of life; and here have I been run down by that self-same water-cart, and my leg is broken."

"Dear me!" said the physician. "This is very sad. But I perceive I must explain to you the action of my paint. A broken bone is a mighty small affair at the worst of it; and it belongs to a class of accident to which my paint is quite inapplicable. Sin, my dear young friend, sin is the sole calamity that a wise man should apprehend; it is against sin that I have fitted you out; and when you come to be tempted, you will give me news of my paint."

"Oh!" said the young man, "I did not understand that, and it seems rather disappointing. But I have no doubt all is for the best; and in the meanwhile, I shall be obliged to you if you will set my leg."

"That is none of my business," said the physician; "but if your bearers will carry you round the corner to the surgeon's, I feel sure he will afford relief."

Some three years later, the young man came running to the physician's house in a great perturbation. "What is the meaning of this?" he cried. "Here was I to be set free from the bondage of sin; and I have just committed forgery, arson and murder."

"Dear me," said the physician. "This is very serious. Off with your clothes at once." And as soon as the young man had stripped, he examined him from head to foot. "No," he cried with great relief, "there is not a flake broken. Cheer up, my young friend, your paint is as good as new."

"Good God!" cried the young man, "and what then can be the use of it?"

"Why," said the physician, "I perceive I must explain to you the nature of the action of my paint. It does not exactly prevent sin; it extenuates instead the painful conse-quences. It is not so much for this world, as for the next; it is not against life; in short, it is against death that I have fitted you out. And when you come to die, you will give me news of my paint."

"Oh!" cried the young man, "I had not understood that, and it seems a little disap-pointing. But there is no doubt all is for the best: and in the meanwhile, I shall be obliged if you will help me to undo the evil I have brought on innocent persons."

"That is none of my business," said the physician; "but if you will go round the corner to the police office, I feel sure it will afford you relief to give yourself up."

Six weeks later, the physician was called to the town gaol.

"What is the meaning of this?" cried the young man. "Here am I literally crusted with your paint; and I have broken my leg, and committed all the crimes in the calendar, and must be hanged to-morrow; and am in the meanwhile in a fear so extreme that I lack words to picture it."

"Dear me," said the physician. "This is really amazing. Well, well; perhaps, if you had not been painted, you would have been more frightened still."

VIII.

THE HOUSE OF ELD.

So soon as the child began to speak, the gyve was riveted; and the boys and girls limped about their play like convicts. Doubtless it was more pitiable to see and more painful to bear in youth; but even the grown folk, besides being very unhandy on their feet, were often sick with ulcers.

About the time when Jack was ten years old, many strangers began to journey through that country. These he beheld going lightly by on the long roads, and the thing amazed him. "I wonder how it comes," he asked, "that all these strangers are so quick afoot, and we must drag about our fetter?"

"My dear boy," said his uncle, the catechist, "do not complain about your fetter, for it is the only thing that makes life worth living. None are happy, none are good, none are respectable, that are not gyved like us. And I must tell you, besides, it is very dangerous talk. If you grumble of your iron, you will have no luck; if ever you take it off, you will be instantly smitten by a thunderbolt."

"Are there no thunderbolts for these strangers?" asked Jack.

"Jupiter is longsuffering to the be‹ nighted," returned the catechist.

"Upon my word, I could wish I had been less fortunate," said Jack. "For if I had been born benighted, I might now be going free; and it cannot be denied the iron is inconvenient, and the ulcer hurts."

"Ah!" cried his uncle, "do not envy the heathen! Theirs is a sad lot! Ah, poor souls, if they but knew the joys of being fettered! Poor souls, my heart yearns for them. But the truth is they are vile, odious, insolent, ill-conditioned, stinking brutes, not truly human—for what is a man without a

12

fetter?—and you cannot be too particular not to touch or speak with them."

After this talk, the child would never pass one of the unfettered on the road but what he spat at him and called him names, which was the practice of the children in that part.

It chanced one day, when he was fifteen, he went into the woods, and the ulcer pained him. It was a fair day, with a blue sky; all the birds were singing; but Jack nursed his foot. Presently, another song began; it sounded like the singing of a person, only far more gay; at the same time there was a beating on the earth. Jack put aside the leaves; and there was a lad of his own village, leaping, and dancing and singing to himself in a green dell; and on the grass beside him lay the dancer's iron.

"Oh!" cried Jack, "you have your fetter off!"

"For God's sake, don't tell your uncle!" cried the lad.

"If you fear my uncle," returned Jack "why do you not fear the thunderbolt"?

" That is only an old wives' tale," said the other. " It is only told to children. Scores of us come here among the woods and dance for nights together, and are none the worse."

This put Jack in a thousand new thoughts. He was a grave lad; he had no mind to dance himself; he wore his fetter manfully, and tended his ulcer without complaint. But he loved the less to be deceived or to see others cheated. He began to lie in wait for heathen travellers, at covert parts of the road, and in the dusk of the day, so that he might speak with them unseen; and these were greatly taken with their wayside ques-tioner, and told him things of weight. The wearing of gyves (they said) was no com-mand of Jupiter's. It was the contrivance of a white-faced thing, a sorcerer, that dwelt in that country in the Wood of Eld. He was one like Glaucus that could change his shape, yet he could be always told; for when he was crossed, he gobbled like a turkey. He had three lives; but the third smiting would make an end of him indeed; and with that his house of sorcery would vanish, the gyves fall, and the villagers take hands and dance like children.

"And in your country?" Jack would ask.

But at this the travellers, with one accord, would put him off; until Jack began to suppose there was no land entirely happy. Or, if there were, it must be one that kept its folk at home; which was natural enough.

But the case of the gyves weighed upon him. The sight of the children limping stuck in his eyes; the groans of such as dressed their ulcers haunted him. And it came at last in his mind that he was born to free them.

There was in that village a sword of heavenly forgery, beaten upon Vulcan's anvil. It was never used but in the temple, and then the flat of it only; and it hung on a nail by the catechist's chimney. Early one night, Jack rose, and took the sword, and was gone out of the house and the village in the darkness.

All night he walked at a venture; and when day came, he met strangers going to the fields. Then he asked after the Wood of Eld and the house of sorcery; and one said north, and one south; until Jack saw that they deceived him. So then, when he asked his way of any man, he showed the bright sword naked; and at that the gyve on the man's ankle rang, and answered in his stead; and the word was still *Straight on.* But the man, when his gyve spoke, spat and struck at Jack, and threw stones at him as he went away; so that his head was broken.

So he came to that wood, and entered in, and he was aware of a house in a low place, where funguses grew, and the trees met, and the steaming of the marsh arose about it like a smoke. It was a fine house, and a very rambling; some parts of it were ancient like the hills, and some but of yesterday, and none finished; and all the ends of it were open, so that you could go in from every side. Yet it was in good repair, and all the chimneys smoked.

Jack went in through the gable; and there was one room after another, all bare, but all furnished in part, so that a man could dwell there; and in each there was a fire burning, where a man could warm himself, and a table spread where he might eat. But Jack saw nowhere any living creature; only the bodies of some stuffed.

"This is a hospitable house," said Jack; "but the ground must be quaggy underneath, for at every step the building quakes."

He had gone some time in the house, when he began to be hungry. Then he looked at the food, and at first he was afraid; but he bared the sword, and by the shining of the sword, it seemed the food was honest. So he took the courage to sit down and eat, and he was refreshed in mind and body.

"This is strange," thought he, "that in the house of sorcery there should be food so wholesome."

As he was yet eating, there came into that room the appearance of his uncle, and Jack was afraid because he had taken the sword. But his uncle was never more kind, and sat down to meat with him, and praised him because he had taken the sword. Never had these two been more pleasantly together, and Jack was full of love to the man.

" It was very well done," said his uncle, "to take the sword and come yourself into the House of Eld; a good thought and a brave deed. But now you are satisfied; and we may go home to dinner arm in arm."

"Oh, dear, no!" said Jack. "I am not satisfied yet."

"How!" cried his uncle. "Are you not warmed by the fire? Does not this food sustain you?"

"I see the food to be wholesome," said Jack; "and still it is no proof that a man should wear a gyve on his right leg."

Now at this the appearance of his uncle gobbled like a turkey.

"Jupiter!" cried Jack, "is this the sorcerer?"

His hand held back and his heart failed him for the love he bore his uncle; but he heaved up the sword and smote the appearance on the head; and it cried out aloud with the voice of his uncle; and fell to the ground; and a little bloodless white thing fled from the room.

The cry rang in Jack's ears, and his knees smote together, and conscience cried upon him; and yet he was strengthened, and there woke in his bones the lust of that enchanter's blood. "If the gyves are to fall," said he, "I must go through with this, and when I get home I shall find my uncle dancing."

So he went on after the bloodless thing. In the way, he met the appearance of his father; and his father was incensed, and railed upon him, and called to him upon his duty, and bade him be home, while there was yet time. "For you can still," said he, "be home by sunset; and then all will be forgiven."

"God knows," said Jack, "I fear your anger; but yet your anger does not prove that a man should wear a gyve on his right leg."

And at that the appearance of his father gobbled like a turkey.

"Ah, heaven," cried Jack, "the sorcerer again!"

The blood ran backward in his body and his joints rebelled against him for the love he bore his father; but he heaved up the sword, and plunged it in the heart of the appearance; and the appearance cried out aloud with the voice of his father; and fell to the ground; and a little bloodless white thing fled from the room.

The cry rang in Jack's ears, and his soul was darkened; but now rage came to him. "I have done what I dare not think upon," said he. "I will go to an end with it, or perish. And when I get home, I pray God this may be a dream, and I may find my father dancing."

So he went on after the bloodless thing

that had escaped; and in the way he met the appearance of his mother, and she wept. "What have you done?" she cried. "What is this that you have done? Oh, come home (where you may be by bedtime) ere you do more ill to me and mine; for it is enough to smite my brother and your father."

"Dear mother, it is not these that I have smitten," said Jack; "it was but the enchanter in their shape. And even if I had, it would not prove that a man should wear a gyve on his right leg."

And at this the appearance gobbled like a turkey.

He never knew how he did that; but he swung the sword on the one side, and clove the appearance through the midst; and it cried out aloud with the voice of his mother; and fell to the ground; and with the fall of it, the house was gone from over Jack's head, and he stood alone in the woods, and the gyve was loosened from his leg.

"Well," said he, "the enchanter is now dead, and the fetter gone." But the cries rang in his soul, and the day was like night to him. "This has been a sore business," said he. "Let me get forth out of the wood, and see the good that I have done to others."

He thought to leave the fetter where it lay, but when he turned to go, his mind was otherwise. So he stooped and put the gyve in his bosom; and the rough iron galled him as he went, and his bosom bled.

Now when he was forth of the wood upon the highway, he met folk returning from the field; and those he met had no fetter on the right leg, but, behold! they had one upon the left. Jack asked them what it signified; and they said, "that was the new wear, for the old was found to be a superstition". Then he looked at them nearly; and there was a new ulcer on the left ankle, and the old one on the right was not yet healed.

"Now, may God forgive me!" cried Jack. "I would I were well home."

And when he was home, there lay his uncle smitten on the head, and his father pierced through the heart, and his mother cloven through the midst. And he sat in the lone house and wept beside the bodies.

MORAL.

Old is the tree and the fruit good,
Very old and thick the wood.
Woodman, is your courage stout?
Beware! the root is wrapped about
Your mother's heart, your father's bones:
And like the mandrake comes with groans.

IX

THE FOUR REFORMERS.

FOUR reformers met under a bramble bush. They were all agreed the world must be changed. "We must abolish property," said one.

"We must abolish marriage," said the second.

"We must abolish God," said the third.

"I wish we could abolish work," said the fourth.

"Do not let us get beyond practical politics," said the first. "The first thing is to reduce men to a common level."

"The first thing," said the second, "is to give freedom to the sexes."

"The first thing," said the third, "is to find out how to do it."

" The first step," said the first, "is to abolish the Bible."

" The first thing," said the second, "is to abolish the laws."

" The first thing," said the third, "is to abolish mankind."

X.

THE MAN AND HIS FRIEND.

A MAN quarrelled with his friend.

"I have been much deceived in you," said the man.

And the friend made a face at him and went away.

A little after, they both died, and came together before the great white Justice of the Peace. It began to look black for the friend, but the man for a while had a clear character and was getting in good spirits.

"I find here some record of a quarrel," said the justice, looking in his notes. "Which of you was in the wrong?"

"He was," said the man. "He spoke ill of me behind my back."

"Did he so?" said the justice. "And pray how did he speak about your neighbours?"

" Oh, he had always a nasty tongue," said the man.

" And you chose him for your friend?" cried the justice. " My good fellow, we have no use here for fools."

So the man was cast in the pit, and the friend laughed out aloud in the dark and remained to be tried on other charges.

XI.

THE READER.

" I NEVER read such an impious book," said the reader, throwing it on the floor.

"You need not hurt me," said the book; "you will only get less for me second hand, and I did not write myself."

"That is true," said the reader. "My quarrel is with your author."

"Ah, well," said the book, "you need not buy his rant."

"That is true," said the reader. "But I thought him such a cheerful writer."

"I find him so," said the book.

"You must be differently made from me," said the reader.

"Let me tell you a fable," said the book. "There were two men wrecked upon a desert island; one of them made

believe he was at home, the other admitted ——"

"Oh, I know your kind of fable," said
the reader. "They both died."

"And so they did," said the book. "No
doubt of that. And everybody else."

"That is true," said the reader. "Push
it a little further for this once. And when
they were all dead?"

"They were in God's hands, the same
as before," said the book.

"Not much to boast of, by your account,"
cried the reader.

"Who is impious now?" said the book.
And the reader put him on the fire.

> The coward crouches from the rod,
> And loathes the iron face of God.

XII.

THE CITIZEN AND THE TRAVELLER.

"Look round you," said the citizen. "This is the largest market in the world."

"Oh, surely not," said the traveller.

"Well, perhaps not the largest," said the citizen, "but much the best."

"You are certainly wrong there," said the traveller. "I can tell you . . ."

They buried the stranger at the dusk.

XIII.

THE DISTINGUISHED STRANGER.

ONCE upon a time there came to this earth a visitor from a neighbouring planet. And he was met at the place of his descent by a great philosopher, who was to show him everything.

First of all they came through a wood, and the stranger looked upon the trees. "Whom have we here?" said he.

"These are only vegetables," said the philosopher. "They are alive, but not at all interesting."

"I don't know about that," said the stranger. "They seem to have very good manners. Do they never speak?"

"They lack the gift," said the philosopher.

"Yet I think I hear them sing," said the other.

" That is only the wind among the leaves," said the philosopher. " I will explain to you the theory of winds: it is very interesting."

"Well," said the stranger, "I wish I knew what they are thinking."

"They cannot think," said the philosopher.

" I don't know about that," returned the stranger : and then, laying his hand upon a trunk: " I like these people," said he.

" They are not people at all," said the philosopher. "Come along."

Next they came through a meadow where there were cows.

" These are very dirty people," said the stranger.

" They are not people at all," said the philosopher ; and he explained what a cow is in scientific words which I have forgotten.

" That is all one to me," said the stranger. " But why do they never look up ? "

" Because they are graminivorous," said the philosopher ; "and to live upon grass, which is not highly nutritious, requires so close an attention to business that they have no time to think, or speak, or look at the scenery, or keep themselves clean."

"Well," said the stranger, "that is one way to live, no doubt. But I prefer the people with the green heads."

Next they came into a city, and the streets were full of men and women.

" These are very odd people," said the stranger.

" They are the people of the greatest nation in the world," said the philosopher.

" Are they indeed ? " said the stranger. " They scarcely look so."

XIV.

THE CART-HORSES AND THE SADDLE-HORSE.

Two cart-horses, a gelding and a mare, were brought to Samoa, and put in the same field with a saddle-horse to run free on the island. They were rather afraid to go near him, for they saw he was a saddle-horse, and supposed he would not speak to them. Now the saddle-horse had never seen creatures so big. "These must be great chiefs," thought he, and he approached them civilly. "Lady and gentleman," said he, "I understand you are from the colonies. I offer you my affectionate compliments, and make you heartily welcome to the islands."

The colonials looked at him askance, and consulted with each other.

"Who can he be?" said the gelding.

"He seems suspiciously civil," said **the** mare.

"I do not think he can be much account," said the gelding.

"Depend upon it he is only a Kanaka," said the mare.

Then they turned to him.

"Go to the devil!" said the gelding.

"I wonder at your impudence, speaking to persons of our quality!" cried the mare.

The saddle-horse went away by himself. "I was right," said he, "they are great chiefs."

XV

THE TADPOLE AND THE FROG.

"Be ashamed of yourself," said the frog. "When I was a tadpole, I had no tail."

"Just what I thought!" said the tadpole. "You never were a tadpole."

XVI.

SOMETHING IN IT.

THE natives told him many tales. In particular, they warned him of the house of yellow reeds tied with black sinnet, how any one who touched it became instantly the prey of Akaänga, and was handed on to him by Miru the ruddy, and hocussed with the kava of the dead, and baked in the ovens and eaten by the eaters of the dead.

"There is nothing in it," said the missionary.

There was a bay upon that island, a very fair bay to look upon ; but, by the native saying, it was death to bathe there. "There is nothing in that," said the missionary ; and he came to the bay, and went swimming. Presently an eddy took him and bore him towards the reef. "Oho!" thought the missionary, "it seems there is something in it after all." And he swam the harder, but the eddy carried him away. "I do not care about this eddy," said the missionary; and even as he said it, he was aware of a house raised on piles above the sea; it was built of yellow reeds, one reed joined with another, and the whole bound with black sinnet; a ladder led to the door, and all about the house hung calabashes. He had never seen such a house, nor yet such calabashes; and the eddy set for the ladder. "This is singular," said the missionary, "but there can be nothing in it." And he laid hold of the ladder and went up. It was a fine house; but there was no man there; and when the missionary looked back he saw no island, only the heaving of the sea. "It is strange about the island," said the missionary, "but who's afraid? my stories are the true ones." And he laid hold of a calabash, for he was one that loved curiosities. Now he had no sooner laid hand upon the calabash than that which he handled, and that which he saw and stood on, burst like a bubble and was gone; and night closed upon him, and the waters, and the meshes of the net; and he wallowed there like a fish.

"A body would think there was something in this," said the missionary. "But if these tales are true, I wonder what about my tales!"

Now the flaming of Akaänga's torch drew near in the night; and the misshapen hands groped in the meshes of the net; and they took the missionary between the finger and the thumb, and bore him dripping in the night and silence to the place of the ovens of Miru. And there was Miru, ruddy in the glow of the ovens; and there sat her four daughters, and made the kava of the dead; and there sat the comers out of the islands of the living, dripping and lamenting.

This was a dread place to reach for any of the sons of men. But of all who ever came there, the missionary was the most concerned; and, to make things worse, the person next him was a convert of his own.

"Aha," said the convert, "so you are here like your neighbours? And how about all your stories?"

"It seems," said the missionary, with bursting tears, "that there was nothing in them."

By this the kava of the dead was ready, and the daughters of Miru began to intone in the old manner of singing. "Gone are the green islands and the bright sea, the sun and the moon and the forty million stars, and life and love and hope. Henceforth is no more, only to sit in the night and silence, and see your friends devoured; for life is a deceit, and the bandage is taken from your eyes."

Now when the singing was done, one of the daughters came with the bowl. Desire of that kava rose in the missionary's bosom; he lusted for it like a swimmer for the land, or a bridegroom for his bride; and he reached out his hand, and took the bowl, and would have drunk. And then he remembered, and put it back.

"Drink!" sang the daughter of Miru.

"There is no kava like the kava of the dead, and to drink of it once is the reward of living."

"I thank you. It smells excellent," said the missionary. "But I am a blue-ribbon man myself; and though I am aware there is a difference of opinion even in our own confession, I have always held kava to be excluded."

"What!" cried the convert. "Are you going to respect a taboo at a time like this? And you were always so opposed to taboos when you were alive!"

"To other people's," said the missionary. "Never to my own."

"But yours have all proved wrong," said the convert.

"It looks like it," said the missionary, "and I can't help that. No reason why I should break my word."

"I never heard the like of this!" cried the daughter of Miru. "Pray, what do you expect to gain?"

"That is not the point," said the missionary. " I took this pledge for others, I am not going to break it for myself."

The daughter of Miru was puzzled ; she came and told her mother, and Miru was vexed ; and they went and told Akaänga.

" I don't know what to do about this," said Akaänga ; and he came and reasoned with the missionary.

" But there *is* such a thing as right and wrong," said the missionary ; "and your ovens cannot alter that."

" Give the kava to the rest," said Akaänga to the daughters of Miru. " I must get rid of this sea-lawyer instantly, or worse will come of it."

The next moment the missionary came up in the midst of the sea, and there before him were the palm trees of the island. He swam to the shore gladly, and landed. Much matter of thought was in that missionary's mind.

" I seem to have been misinformed upon some points," said he. " Perhaps there is not much in it, as I supposed ; but there is something in it after all. Let me be glad of that."

And he rang the bell for service.

MORAL.

The sticks break, the stones crumble,
The eternal altars tilt and tumble,
Sanctions and tales dislimn like mist
About the amazed evangelist.
He stands unshook from age to youth
Upon one pin-point of the truth.

XVII.

FAITH, HALF FAITH AND NO FAITH AT ALL.

In the ancient days there went three men upon pilgrimage; one was a priest, and one was a virtuous person, and the third was an old rover with his axe.

As they went, the priest spoke about the grounds of faith.

"We find the proofs of our religion in the works of nature," said he, and beat his breast.

"That is true," said the virtuous person.

"The peacock has a scrannel voice," said the priest, "as has been laid down always in our books How cheering!" he cried, in a voice like one that wept. "How comforting!"

"I require no such proofs," said the virtuous person.

" Then you have no reasonable faith," said the priest.

" Great is the right, and shall prevail!" cried the virtuous person. " There is loyalty in my soul; be sure, there is loyalty in the mind of Odin."

" These are but playings upon words," returned the priest. " A sackful of such trash is nothing to the peacock."

Just then they passed a country farm. where there was a peacock seated on a rail; and the bird opened its mouth and sang with the voice of a nightingale.

" Where are you now?" asked the virtuous person. " And yet this shakes not me! Great is the truth, and shall prevail!"

" The devil fly away with that peacock!" said the priest; and he was downcast for a mile or two.

But presently they came to a shrine, where a Fakeer performed miracles.

" Ah!" said the priest, " here are the true grounds of faith. The peacock was but an adminicle   This is the base of our religion."

And he beat upon his breast, and groaned like one with colic.

" Now to me," said the virtuous person, " all this is as little to the purpose as the peacock. I believe because I see the right is great and must prevail; and this Fakeer might carry on with his conjuring tricks till doomsday, and it would not play bluff upon a man like me."

Now at this the Fakeer was so much incensed that his hand trembled; and, lo! in the midst of a miracle the cards fell from up his sleeve.

"Where are you now?" asked the virtuous person. "And yet it shakes not me!"

" The devil fly away with the Fakeer!" cried the priest. " I really do not see the good of going on with this pilgrimage."

" Cheer up!" cried the virtuous person. " Great is the right, and shall prevail!"

" If you are quite sure it will prevail," says the priest.

" I pledge my word for that," said the virtuous person.

So the other began to go on again with a better heart.

At last one came running, and told them all was lost : that the powers of darkness had besieged the Heavenly Mansions, that Odin was to die, and evil triumph.

" I have been grossly deceived," cried the virtuous person.

" All is lost now," said the priest.

" I wonder if it is too late to make it up with the devil?" said the virtuous person.

" Oh, I hope not," said the priest. " And at any rate we can but try. But what are you doing with your axe?" says he to the rover.

" I am off to die with Odin," said the rover.

XVIII.

THE TOUCHSTONE.

THE King was a man that stood well before the world; his smile was sweet as clover, but his soul withinsides was as little as a pea. He had two sons; and the younger son was a boy after his heart, but the elder was one whom he feared. It befell one morning that the drum sounded in the dun before it was yet day; and the King rode with his two sons, and a brave array behind them. They rode two hours, and came to the foot of a brown mountain that was very steep.

"Where do we ride?" said the elder son.

"Across this brown mountain." said the King, and smiled to himself.

"My father knows what he is doing," said the younger son.

And they rode two hours more, and
came to the sides of a black river that was
wondrous deep.

" And where do we ride ? " asked the
elder son.

" Over this black river," said the King,
and smiled to himself.

" My father knows what he is doing,"
said the younger son.

And they rode all that day, and about
the time of the sunsetting came to the side
of a lake, where was a great dun.

" It is here we ride," said the King ;
" to a King's house, and a priest's, and a
house where you will learn much."

At the gates of -the dun, the King who
was a priest met them ; and he was a grave
man, and beside him stood his daughter,
and she was as fair as the morn, and one
that smiled and looked down.

" These are my two sons," said the first
King.

" And here is my daughter," said the King
who was a priest.

"She is a wonderful fine maid," said the first King, "and I like her manner of smiling."

"They are wonderful well-grown lads," said the second, "and I like their gravity."

And then the two Kings looked at each other, and said, "The thing may come about".

And in the meanwhile the two lads looked upon the maid, and the one grew pale and the other red; and the maid looked upon the ground smiling.

"Here is the maid that I shall marry," said the elder. "For I think she smiled upon me."

But the younger plucked his father by the sleeve. "Father," said he, "a word in your ear. If I find favour in your sight, might not I wed this maid, for I think she smiles upon me?"

"A word in yours," said the King his father. "Waiting is good hunting, and when the teeth are shut the tongue is at home."

Now they were come into the dun, and
feasted ; and this was a great house, so that
the lads were astonished ; and the King that
was a priest sat at the end of the board and
was silent, so that the lads were filled with
reverence; and the maid served them smiling with downcast eyes, so that their hearts
were enlarged.

Before it was day, the elder son arose, and
he found the maid at her weaving, for she
was a diligent girl. " Maid," quoth he, " I
would fain marry you."

"You must speak with my father," said
she, and she looked upon the ground smiling, and became like the rose.

" Her heart is with me," said the elder
son, and he went down to the lake and
sang.

A little after came the younger son.
" Maid," quoth he, "if our fathers were
agreed, I would like well to marry you."

"You can speak to my father," said she ;
and looked upon the ground, and smiled and
grew like the rose.

"She is a dutiful daughter," said the younger son, "she will make an obedient wife." And then he thought, "What shall I do?" and he remembered the King her father was a priest; so he went into the temple, and sacrificed a weasel and a hare.

Presently the news got about; and the two lads and the first King were called into the presence of the King who was a priest, where he sat upon the high seat.

"Little I reck of gear," said the King who was a priest, "and little of power. For we live here among the shadow of things, and the heart is sick of seeing them. And we stay here in the wind like raiment drying, and the heart is weary of the wind. But one thing I love, and that is truth; and for one thing will I give my daughter, and that is the trial stone. For in the light of that stone the seeming goes, and the being shows, and all things besides are worthless. Therefore, lads, if ye would wed my daughter, out foot, and bring me the stone of touch, for that is the price of her."

"A word in your ear," said the younger son to his father. "I think we do very well without this stone."

"A word in yours," said the father. "I am of your way of thinking; but when the teeth are shut the tongue is at home." And he smiled to the King that was a priest.

But the elder son got to his feet, and called the King that was a priest by the name of father. "For whether I marry the maid or no, I will call you by that word for the love of your wisdom; and even now I will ride forth and search the world for the stone of touch." So he said farewell, and rode into the world.

"I think I will go, too," said the younger son, "if I can have your leave. For my heart goes out to the maid."

"You will ride home with me," said his father.

So they rode home, and when they came to the dun, the King had his son into his treasury. "Here," said he, "is the touch-stone which shows truth; for there is no truth but plain truth; and if you will look in this, you will see yourself as you are."

And the younger son looked in it, and saw his face as it were the face of a beardless youth, and he was well enough pleased; for the thing was a piece of a mirror.

"Here is no such great thing to make a work about," said he; "but if it will get me the maid I shall never complain. But what a fool is my brother to ride into the world, and the thing all the while at home!"

So they rode back to the other dun, and showed the mirror to the King that was a priest; and when he had looked in it, and seen himself like a King, and his house like a King's house, and all things like themselves, he cried out and blessed God. "For now I know," said he, "there is no truth but the plain truth; and I am a King indeed, although my heart misgave me." And he pulled down his temple, and built a new one; and then the younger son was married to the maid.

In the meantime the elder son rode into

the world to find the touchstone of the trial
of truth ; and whenever he came to a place
of habitation, he would ask the men if they
had heard of it. And in every place the
men answered : " Not only have we heard
of it, but we alone, of all men, possess the
thing itself, and it hangs in the side of our
chimney to this day ". Then would the
elder son be glad, and beg for a sight of it.
And sometimes it would be a piece of mirror,
that showed the seeming of things ; and then
he would say, " This can never be, for
there should be more than seeming ". And
sometimes it would be a lump of coal,
which showed nothing ; and then he would
say, " This can never be, for at least there
is the seeming ". And sometimes it would
be a touchstone indeed, beautiful in hue,
adorned with polishing, the light inhabiting
its sides ; and when he found this, he would
beg the thing, and the persons of that place
would give it him, for all men were very
generous of that gift ; so that at the last
he had his wallet full of them, and they

chinked together when he rode ; and when he halted by the side of the way he would take them out and try them, till his head turned like the sails upon a windmill.

"A murrain upon this business!" said the elder son, "for I perceive no end to it. Here I have the red, and here the blue and the green ; and to me they seem all excellent, and yet shame each other. A murrain on the trade! If it were not for the King that is a priest and whom I have called my father, and if it were not for the fair maid of the dun that makes my mouth to sing and my heart enlarge, I would even tumble them all into the salt sea, and go home and be a King like other folk."

But he was like the hunter that has seen a stag upon a mountain, so that the night may fall, and the fire be kindled, and the lights shine in his house ; but desire of that stag is single in his bosom.

Now after many years the elder son came upon the sides of the salt sea ; and it was night, and a savage place, and the clamour of

the sea was loud.   There he was aware of a
house, and a man that sat there by the light
of a candle, for he had no fire   Now the
elder son came in to him, and the man gave
him water to drink, for he had no bread;
and wagged his head when he was spoken
to, for he had no words.

"Have you the touchstone of truth?"
asked the elder son; and when the man
had wagged his head, "I might have known
that," cried the elder son. "I have here a
wallet full of them!" And with that he
laughed, although his heart was weary.

And with that the man laughed too, and with
the fuff of his laughter the candle went out.

"Sleep," said the man, "for now I think
you have come far enough; and your quest
is ended, and my candle is out."

Now when the morning came, the man
gave him a clear pebble in his hand, and it
had no beauty and no colour; and the elder
son looked upon it scornfully and shook his
head; and he went away, for it seemed a
small affair to him.

All that day he rode, and his mind was quiet, and the desire of the chase allayed. " How if this poor pebble be the touchstone, after all?" said he: and he got down from his horse, and emptied forth his wallet by the side of the way. Now, in the light of each other, all the touchstones lost their hue and fire, and withered like stars at morning; but in the light of the pebble, their beauty remained, only the pebble was the most bright. And the elder son smote upon his brow. " How if this be the truth?" he cried, " that all are a little true?" And he took the pebble, and turned its light upon the heavens, and they deepened about him like the pit; and he turned it on the hills, and the hills were cold and rugged, but life ran in their sides so that his own life bounded; and he turned it on the dust, and he beheld the dust with joy and terror; and he turned it on himself, and kneeled down and prayed.

" Now, thanks be to God," said the elder son, " I have found the touchstone; and now I may turn my reins, and ride home to the

King and to the maid of the dun that makes my mouth to sing and my heart enlarge."

Now when he came to the dun, he saw children playing by the gate where the King had met him in the old days; and this stayed his pleasure, for he thought in his heart, " It is here my children should be playing". And when he came into the hall, there was his brother on the high seat and the maid beside him; and at that his anger rose, for he thought in his heart, " It is I that should be sitting there, and the maid beside me".

" Who are you? " said his brother. " And what make you in the dun? "

" I am your elder brother," he replied. " And I am come to marry the maid, for I have brought the touchstone of truth."

Then the younger brother laughed aloud. " Why," said he, " I found the touchstone years ago, and married the maid, and there are our children playing at the gate."

Now at this the elder brother grew as gray as the dawn " I pray you have dealt justly," said he, "for I perceive my life is lost."

"Justly?" quoth the younger brother. "It becomes you ill, that are a restless man and a runagate, to doubt my justice, or the King my father's, that are sedentary folk and known in the land."

"Nay," said the elder brother, "you have all else, have patience also; and suffer me to say the world is full of touchstones, and it appears not easily which is true."

"I have no shame of mine," said the younger brother. "There it is, and look in it."

So the elder brother looked in the mirror, and he was sore amazed; for he was an old man, and his hair was white upon his head; and he sat down in the hall and wept aloud.

"Now," said the younger brother, "see what a fool's part you have played, that ran over all the world to seek what was lying in our father's treasury, and came back an old carle for the dogs to bark at, and without chick or child. And I that was dutiful and

15

wise sit here crowned with virtues and pleasures, and happy in the light of my hearth."

"Methinks you have a cruel tongue," said the elder brother; and he pulled out the clear pebble and turned its light on his brother; and behold the man was lying, his soul was shrunk into the smallness of a pea, and his heart was a bag of little fears like scorpions, and love was dead in his bosom. And at that the elder brother cried out aloud, and turned the light of the pebble on the maid, and, lo! she was but a mask of a woman, and withinsides she was quite dead, and she smiled as a clock ticks, and knew not wherefore.

"Oh, well," said the elder brother, "I perceive there is both good and bad. So fare ye all as well as ye may in the dun; but I will go forth into the world with my pebble in my pocket."

XIX.

THE POOR THING.

THERE was a man in the islands who fished for his bare bellyful, and took his life in his hands to go forth upon the sea between four planks. But though he had much ado, he was merry of heart; and the gulls heard him laugh when the spray met him. And though he had little lore, he was sound of spirit; and when the fish came to his hook in the mid-waters, he blessed God without weighing. He was bitter poor in goods and bitter ugly of countenance, and he had no wife.

It fell in the time of the fishing that the man awoke in his house about the midst of the afternoon. The fire burned in the midst, and the smoke went up and the sun came down by the chimney. And the man was

aware of the likeness of one that warmed
his hands at the red peats.

"I greet you," said the man, "in the
name of God."

"I greet you," said he that warmed his
hands, "but not in the name of God, for I
am none of His; nor in the name of Hell, for
I am not of Hell.   For I am but a bloodless
thing, less than wind and lighter than a
sound, and the wind goes through me like
a net, and I am broken by a sound and
shaken by the cold."

"Be plain with me," said the man, "and
tell me your name and of your nature."

"My name," quoth the other, "is not yet
named, and my nature not yet sure.   For I
am part of a man; and I was a part of your
fathers, and went out to fish and fight with
them in the ancient days.   But now is my
turn not yet come; and I wait until you have
a wife, and then shall I be in your son, and
a brave part of him, rejoicing manfully
to launch the boat into the surf, skilful to
direct the helm, and a man of might

where the ring closes and the blows are going."

"This is a marvellous thing to hear," said the man ; "and if you are indeed to be my son, I fear it will go ill with you ; for I am bitter poor in goods and bitter ugly in face, and I shall never get me a wife if I live to the age of eagles."

"All this have I come to remedy, my Father," said the Poor Thing ; "for we must go this night to the little isle of sheep, where our fathers lie in the dead-cairn, and to-morrow to the Earl's Hall, and there shall you find a wife by my providing."

So the man rose and put forth his boat at the time of the sunsetting ; and the Poor Thing sat in the prow, and the spray blew through his bones like snow, and the wind whistled in his teeth, and the boat dipped not with the weight of him.

"I am fearful to see you, my son," said the man. "For methinks you are no thing of God."

"It is only **the** wind that whistles in my

teeth," said the Poor Thing, " and there is no life in me to keep it out."

So they came to the little isle of sheep, where the surf burst all about it in the midst of the sea, and it was all green with bracken, and all wet with dew, and the moon enlightened it. They ran the boat into a cove, and set foot to land; and the man came heavily behind among the rocks in the deepness of the bracken, but the Poor Thing went before him like a smoke in the light of the moon. So they came to the dead-cairn, and they laid their ears to the stones; and the dead complained withinsides like a swarm of bees: " Time was that marrow was in our bones, and strength in our sinews; and the thoughts of our head were clothed upon with acts and the words of men. But now are we broken in sunder, and the bonds of our bones are loosed, and our thoughts lie in the dust."

Then said the Poor Thing : " Charge them that they give you the virtue they withheld "

And the man said: "Bones of my fathers, greeting! for I am sprung of your loins. And now, behold, I break open the piled stones of your cairn, and I let in the noon between your ribs. Count it well done, for it was to be; and give me what I come seeking in the name of blood and in the name of God."

And the spirits of the dead stirred in the cairn like ants; and they spoke: "You have broken the roof of our cairn and let in the noon between our ribs; and you have the strength of the still-living. But what virtue have we? what power? or what jewel here in the dust with us, that any living man should covet or receive it? for we are less than nothing. But we tell you one thing, speaking with many voices like bees, that the way is plain before all like the grooves of launching: So forth into life and fear not, for so did we all in the ancient ages." And their voices passed away like an eddy in a river.

"Now," said the Poor Thing, "they have

told you a lesson, but make them give you a gift. Stoop your hand among the bones without drawback, and you shall find their treasure."

So the man stooped his hand, and the dead laid hold upon it many and faint like ants; but he shook them off, and behold, what he brought up in his hand was the shoe of a horse, and it was rusty.

" It is a thing of no price," quoth the man, " for it is rusty."

" We shall see that," said the Poor Thing ; " for in my thought it is a good thing to do what our fathers did, and to keep what they kept without question. And in my thought one thing is as good as another in this world ; and a shoe of a horse will do."

Now they got into their boat with the horseshoe, and when the dawn was come they were aware of the smoke of the Earl's town and the bells of the Kirk that beat. So they set foot to shore ; and the man went up to the market among the fishers over against the palace and the Kirk ; and he was bitter poor and bitter ugly, and he had never a fish to sell, but only a shoe of a horse in his creel, and it rusty.

"Now," said the Poor Thing, "do so and so, and you shall find a wife and I a mother."

It befell that the Earl's daughter came forth to go into the Kirk upon her prayers; and when she saw the poor man stand in the market with only the shoe of a horse, and it rusty, it came in her mind it should be a thing of price.

"What is that?" quoth she.

"It is a shoe of a horse," said the man.

"And what is the use of it?" quoth the Earl's daughter.

"It is for no use," said the man.

"I may not believe that," said she; "else why should you carry it?"

"I do so," said he, "because it was so my fathers did in the ancient ages; and I have neither a better reason nor a worse."

Now the Earl's daughter could not find it in her mind to believe him. "Come," quoth she, "sell me this, for I am sure it is a thing of price."

"Nay," said the man, "the thing is not for sale."

"What!" cried the Earl's daughter. "Then what make you here in the town's market, with the thing in your creel and nought beside?"

"I sit here," says the man, "to get me a wife."

"There is no sense in any of these answers," thought the Earl's daughter; "and I could find it in my heart to weep."

By came the Earl upon that; and she called him and told him all. And when he had heard, he was of his daughter's mind that this should be a thing of virtue; and charged the man to set a price upon the thing, or else be hanged upon the gallows; and that was near at hand, so that the man could see it.

"The way of life is straight like the grooves of launching," quoth the man. "And if I am to be hanged let me be hanged."

"Why!" cried the Earl, "will you set your neck against a shoe of a horse, and it rusty?"

"In my thought," said the man, "one thing is as good as another in this world; and a shoe of a horse will do."

"This can never be," thought the Earl; and he stood and looked upon the man, and bit his beard.

And the man looked up at him and smiled. "It was so my fathers did in the ancient ages," quoth he to the Earl, "and I have neither a better reason nor a worse."

"There is no sense in any of this," thought the Earl, "and I must be growing old." So he had his daughter on one side, and says he: "Many suitors have you denied, my child. But here is a very strange matter that a man should cling so to a shoe of a horse, and it rusty; and that he should offer it like a thing on sale, and yet not sell it; and that he should sit there seeking a wife. If I come not to the bottom of this thing, I shall have no more pleasure in bread; and I can see no way, but either I should hang or you should marry him."

"By my troth, but he is bitter ugly," said the Earl's daughter. "How if the gallows be so near at hand?"

"It was not so," said the Earl, "that my fathers did in the ancient ages. I am like the man, and can give you neither a better reason nor a worse. But do you, prithee, speak with him again."

So the Earl's daughter spoke to the man. "If you were not so bitter ugly," quoth she, "my father the Earl would have us marry."

"Bitter ugly am I," said the man, "and you as fair as May. Bitter ugly I am, and what of that? It was so my fathers——"

"In the name of God," said the Earl's daughter, "let your fathers be!"

"If I had done that," said the man, "you had never been chaffering with me here in the market, nor your father the Earl watching with the end of his eye."

"But come," quoth the Earl's daughter,

"this is a very strange thing, that you would have me wed for a shoe of a horse, and it rusty."

"In my thought," quoth the man, "one thing is as good——"

"Oh, spare me that," said the Earl's daughter, "and tell me why I should marry."

"Listen and look," said the man.

Now the wind blew through the Poor Thing like an infant crying, so that her heart was melted; and her eyes were unsealed, and she was aware of the thing as it were a babe unmothered, and she took it to her arms, and it melted in her arms like the air.

"Come," said the man, "behold a vision of our children, the busy hearth, and the white heads. And let that suffice, for it is all God offers."

"I have no delight in it," said she; but with that she sighed.

"The ways of life are straight like the grooves of launching," said the man; and he took her by the hand.

"And what shall we do with the horse-shoe?" quoth she.

"I will give it to your father," said the man; "and he can make a kirk and a mill of it for me."

It came to pass in time that the Poor Thing was born; but memory of these matters slept within him, and he knew not that which he had done. But he was a part of the eldest son; rejoicing manfully to launch the boat into the surf, skilful to direct the helm, and a man of might where the ring closes and the blows are going.

XX.

THE SONG OF THE MORROW.

THE King of Duntrine had a daughter when he was old, and she was the fairest King's daughter between two seas; her hair was like spun gold, and her eyes like pools in a river; and the King gave her a castle upon the sea beach, with a terrace, and a court of the hewn stone, and four towers at the four corners. Here she dwelt and grew up, and had no care for the morrow, and no power upon the hour, after the manner of simple men.

It befell that she walked one day by the beach of the sea, when it was autumn, and the wind blew from the place of rains; and upon the one hand of her the sea beat, and upon the other the dead leaves ran. This was the loneliest beach between

two seas, and strange things had been
done there in the ancient ages. Now the
King's daughter was aware of a crone that
sat upon the beach. The sea foam ran to
her feet, and the dead leaves swarmed
about her back, and the rags blew about
her face in the blowing of the wind.

"Now," said the King's daughter, and
she named a holy name, "this is the most
unhappy old crone between two seas."

"Daughter of a King," said the crone,
"you dwell in a stone house, and your
hair is like the gold: but what is your
profit? Life is not long, nor lives strong;
and you live after the way of simple men,
and have no thought for the morrow and
no power upon the hour."

"Thought for the morrow, that I have,"
said the King's daughter; "but power
upon the hour, that have I not." And she
mused with herself.

Then the crone smote her lean hands
one within the other, and laughed like a
sea-gull. "Home!" cried she. "O daughter

of a King, home to your stone house; for the longing is come upon you now, nor can you live any more after the manner of simple men. Home, and toil and suffer, till the gift come that will make you bare, and till the man come that will bring you care."

The King's daughter made no more ado, but she turned about and went home to her house in silence. And when she was come into her chamber she called for her nurse.

"Nurse," said the King's daughter, "thought is come upon me for the morrow, so that I can live no more after the manner of simple men. Tell me what I must do that I may have power upon the hour."

Then the nurse moaned like a snow wind. "Alas!" said she, "that this thing should be; but the thought is gone into your marrow, nor is there any cure against the thought. Be it so, then, even as you will; though power is less than weakness, power shall you have; and though the thought is colder than winter, yet shall you think it to an end."

So the King's daughter sat in her vaulted
chamber in the masoned house, and she
thought upon the thought. Nine years she
sat ; and the sea beat upon the terrace, and
the gulls cried about the turrets, and wind
crooned in the chimneys of the house. Nine
years she came not abroad, nor tasted the
clean air, neither saw God's sky. Nine
years she sat and looked neither to the right
nor to the left, nor heard speech of any one,
but thought upon the thought of the morrow.
And her nurse fed her in silence, and she
took of the food with her left hand, and ate
it without grace.

Now when the nine years were out, it fell
dusk in the autumn, and there came a sound
in the wind like a sound of piping. At that
the nurse lifted up her finger in the vaulted
house.

"I hear a sound in the wind," said she,
"that is like the sound of piping."

"It is but a little sound," said the King's
daughter, "but yet is it sound enough for
me."

So they went down in the dusk to the
doors of the house, and along the beach of
the sea. And the waves beat upon the one
hand, and upon the other the dead leaves
ran ; and the clouds raced in the sky, and
the gulls flew widdershins. And when they
came to that part of the beach where strange
things had been done in the ancient ages,
lo, there was the crone, and she was dancing
widdershins.

" What makes you dance widdershins, old
crone ? " said the King's daughter ; " here
upon the bleak beach, between the waves
and the dead leaves ? "

" I hear a sound in the wind that is like a
sound of piping," quoth she. " And it is for
that that I dance widdershins. For the gift
comes that will make you bare, and the man
comes that must bring you care. But for
me the morrow is come that I have thought
upon, and the hour of my power."

" How comes it, crone," said the King's
daughter, "that you waver like a rag, and
pale like a dead leaf before my eyes ? "

"Because the morrow has come that I have thought upon, and the hour of my power," said the crone; and she fell on the beach, and, lo! she was but stalks of the sea tangle, and dust of the sea sand, and the sand lice hopped upon the place of her.

"This is the strangest thing that befell between two seas," said the King's daughter of Duntrine.

But the nurse broke out and moaned like an autumn gale. "I am weary of the wind," quoth she; and she bewailed her day.

The King's daughter was aware of a man upon the beach; he went hooded so that none might perceive his face, and a pipe was underneath his arm. The sound of his pipe was like singing wasps, and like the wind that sings in windlestraw; and it took hold upon men's ears like the crying of gulls.

"Are you the comer?" quoth the King's daughter of Duntrine.

"I am the comer," said he, "and these are the pipes that a man may hear, and I have power upon the hour, and this is the song of the morrow." And he piped the song of the morrow, and it was as long as years; and the nurse wept out aloud at the hearing of it.

" This is true," said the King's daughter, " that you pipe the song of the morrow; but that ye have power upon the hour, how may I know that? Show me a marvel here upon the beach, between the waves and the dead leaves."

And the man said, " Upon whom?"

" Here is my nurse," quoth the King's daughter. " She is weary of the wind. Show me a good marvel upon her."

And, lo! the nurse fell upon the beach as it were two handfuls of dead leaves, and the wind whirled them widdershins, and the sand lice hopped between.

" It is true," said the King's daughter of Duntrine; "you are the comer, and you have power upon the hour. Come with me to my stone house."

So they went by the sea margin, and the

man piped the song of the morrow, and the leaves followed behind them as they went. Then they sat down together; and the sea beat on the terrace, and the gulls cried about the towers, and the wind crooned in the chimneys of the house. Nine years they sat, and every year when it fell autumn, the man said, " This is the hour, and I have power in it "; and the daughter of the King said, " Nay, but pipe me the song of the morrow ". And he piped it, and it was long like years.

Now when the nine years were gone, the King's daughter of Duntrine got her to her feet, like one that remembers; and she looked about her in the masoned house; and all her servants were gone; only the man that piped sat upon the terrace with the hand upon his face; and as he piped the leaves ran about the terrace and the sea beat along the wall. Then she cried to him with a great voice, " This is the hour, and let me see the power in it ". And with that the wind blew off the hood from the man's face, and, lo! there was no man there, only the clothes and the hood and the pipes tumbled one upon another in a corner of the terrace, and the dead leaves ran over them.

And the King's daughter of Duntrine got her to that part of the beach where strange things had been done in the ancient ages; and there she sat her down. The sea foam ran to her feet, and the dead leaves swarmed about her back, and the veil blew about her face in the blowing of the wind. And when she lifted up her eyes, there was the daughter of a King come walking on the beach. Her hair was like the spun gold, and her eyes like pools in a river, and she had no thought for the morrow and no power upon the hour, after the manner of simple men.

THE END

ABERDEEN UNIVERSITY PRESS

50074381R10144

Made in the USA
Lexington, KY
26 August 2019